SORCERER'S CHESSMEN

Mark Hansom

RAMBLE HOUSE

ISBN 13: 978-1-60543-342-4

ISBN 10: 1-60543-342-X

Cover Art: Gavin L. O'Keefe
Preparation: Fender Tucker

DANCING TUATARA PRESS #4

MARK HANSOM ABIDES

Welcome to the weird world of Mark Hansom, one of Great Britain's premier authors of the supernatural thriller! As this introduction only appears in the Dancing Tuatara Press edition, you've obviously taken a little trouble to track this book down, as Mr. Hansom's work is somewhat obscure these days, previously (with the exception of *The Beasts of Brahm*) only available in the fantastically rare and expensive original editions. The first editions were all published by Wright and Brown and targeted to the lending library market in the late 1930s. Mellifont reprinted several of the books in brutally truncated form in the early 1950s. So desirable is Hansom's work to collectors that even the abridged volumes command prices of several hundred dollars. Fortunately, the good folks at Ramble House have encouraged me to include all of Hansom's thrillers under the Dancing Tuatara Press imprint.

The world of publishing is a far different creature than it was in the days before WWII, when Hansom was active. Whereas the US market had the pulp magazines, where every variety of thriller had titles devoted to specific sub-genres, the British publishers offered up the much more generic category of "thriller" and produced inexpensive hardcover books for the lending libraries.

Mark Hansom was active in these halcyon days before the folks in marketing had taken over the publishing business and rather than pigeonhole everything into narrow sub-genre categories to make the salespersons' job easier, the broad term of "thriller" was utilized to describe everything from mysteries to supernatural horror to lost race adventures, westerns, and even science fiction. Mark Hansom wrote "thrillers"; mostly of the supernatural variety. His first novel (*The Shadow on the House*) is a masterpiece of psychological horror, and it's only at the denouement that the reader realizes that the implied supernatural activity may well have a rational explanation. I shan't spoil things by telling you which is actually the case, but recommend that you read the novel for yourself, as the book is now available from Ramble House under the Dancing Tuatara Press imprint, and you can read it for yourself. Only one other of his novels was non-supernatural, and is still atmospheric enough that it would have been right at home in one of the US weird menace pulps such as *Horror Stories* or *Thrilling Mystery.*

Hansom's first novel, *The Shadow on the House,* was very well-received, with a US edition being "published" by William Godwin involved swapping out the copyright page and binding up the signatures in the Godwin binding. This first novel has all the atmosphere of the supernatural, but in the end is rationalized, as was his later book, *The Madman.* Other than this one departure, the rest of Hansom's work is fully in the realm of the supernatural and Hansom demonstrates an all-too-rare talent in the genre, the ability to sustain the element of growing dread at novel length.

Hansom pulls this feat in a rather unique manner: He introduces his cast of characters, a fairly conventional cast; you have the hero, his friends, the young damsel who will soon be in distress, and the antagonist; generally a hyper-competent individual with a scientific background who exhibits two common characteristics: (1) He is infatuated with the heroine, regardless of her attachments elsewhere; and (2) Despite his scientific background, he is mucking about with the occult and *things that man was never meant to know . . .*

At first glance these would seem to be the elements of a routine potboiler and nothing that would account for the high esteem that Hansom is held in by those few lucky enough to have read his work. Where Hansom diverges from the routine and carves out his own niche in the annals of supernatural fiction is through a recurring motif that figures in *The Wizard of Berner's Abbey*, *Master of Souls*, *The Ghost of Gaston Revere,* and the present novel, *Sorcerer's Chessmen*". After introducing his antagonist and setting the stage for him to make his first attempt at taking possession of the heroine, Hansom has the villain killed off, generally in the first third of the book!

Where this would seem to be a colossal mistake on the level of Doyle's duel between Holmes and Moriarty at Reichenbach Falls or Michael Moorcock's destruction of not only his protagonist (Elric), but the entire universe at the end of *Stormbringer*; however, in this case Hansom's actually not writing himself into a corner, but is opening the door to having his villain transform from merely human to a force that is far more dangerous in its post-corporeal form. To reveal any more would be to spoil not only the present book, but three of his other novels as well. Suffice it to say, that in each case, Hansom puts an interesting spin on this element that makes each novel a compelling read.

Of his seven novels, his first, *The Shadow on the House* (also available from Ramble House) was named by the late Karl Edward Wagner as one of the thirty-nine best horror novels of all-time, joining such works as *Dracula*, *Fingers of Fear*, *Melmoth the Wanderer*, *The Death Guard*, *Dark Sanctuary* and *Echo of a Curse* . . . Illustrious company indeed! A few years after his article on these books appeared in *Twilight Zone Magazine*, I had occasion to discuss the list with Karl and ventured that in my opinion, as good as The Shadow on the House was, I thought that Hansom had topped it with both *Master of Souls* and *Sorcerer's Chessmen* . . . Karl did go on to acknowledge that at the time of the article, *The Shadow on the House* was the only Hansom novel that he had read. He didn't say whether or not he agreed with my assessment, but it certainly remains a possibility that if he had revisited the list a few years later another Hansom novel or two may well have been added to the list.

So who was this inventive and vastly entertaining author, and why did he stop writing in 1939? The fact of the matter is that no one really knows for certain . . . Even though I was responsible for his entry in the encyclopaedia *Supernatural Literature of the World,* I was unable to include more than a brief bibliography and some conjectures as to what may have become of him . . . We do know that "Mark Hansom" was a pseudonym; there are no records of a person with that name being born (or dying) in the United Kingdom that could have been the author. The man writing as Mark Hansom began his career in 1934 and his career ended almost to the day that Great Britain entered the Second World War. Assuming that he was a young man in mid-to-late twenties at the time it's not at all unreasonable to think that he may have died in the service of his country.

Another possibility is that "Hansom" was the pseudonym for another author working the field, or possibly someone employed in some capacity at Wright & Brown. What suggests this possibility is the program of reprinting abridged versions of his novels undertaken by Mellifont in the 1950s. Certainly it's possible that a contract was entered into by his heirs, but considering the extensive revisions done it would seem more likely that Mellifont had a living author to work with. For what it's worth, the revisions are so brutally cut as to be pretty much incoherent. One simply can't cut a 250-page book to 96 pages and retain anything resembling the power of the original. The fact that some collectors will pay hundreds of dollars for these literary butcheries is baffling to me.

Fortunately, we have *The Beasts of Brahm* in print from Midnight House and this novel and *The Shadow on the House* available from Dancing Tuatara Press, with *The Wizard of Berner's Abbey*, *The Ghost of Gaston Revere*, and *Master of Souls* scheduled to appear in 2010.

John Pelan
Midnight House
2009

SORCERER'S CHESSMEN

CHAPTER I

THE FLAT

THE four men—Mathers, Crossland, Harringay and Forbes—were nervously restless. They were gathered in the dining-room of Forbes' bachelor flat in Regent Street, but, though the room murmured comfort and invited relaxation, none of the men was seated in the orthodox manner.

Forbes, short and dark, stood with one foot on the tiled kerb, and one elbow on the mantel-piece, and gazed into the red heart of the fire. It Harringay, the oldest of the four, a man of fifty, big, ungainly, and with fair hair turning grey, stood behind a settee, gripping the back with outstretched hands. Mathers, little more than a youth, sat on the arm of a leather-upholstered easy chair, continually smoothing his black hair with a nervous movement of his delicate hand, and continually biting his thin, rather cruel-looking lips. Crossland paced the carpet. Crossland was a weedy-looking young man of twenty-five or so, and his nervousness was noticeable even in the tense atmosphere of that room.

Young Mathers leant sideways and reached for his whisky, which stood on the table.

Crossland stopped in his pacing and wheeled about.

"But, dammit! We've got to do something!" he exclaimed.

Forbes, without lifting his dark gaze from the heart of the fire, shrugged his shoulders.

"That's understood," he said in a calm, resonant voice. "We've got to do something."

"Well, it's up to you fellows," said Harringay, stepping round from behind the settee and picking up his whisky from the table. "I've made one suggestion."

He took a gold cigarette-case from the pocket of his dinner jacket, flicked it open and handed it to young Mathers, who was not smoking. Mathers took a cigarette with the barest nod of acknowledgment.

Crossland had resumed his pacing. He stopped again and glanced sulkily at Harringay.

"But we can't *kill* him," he said. "We can't kill a man—"

He was interrupted by the calm voice of Forbes, who still stood gazing into the fire.

"Why can't we?"

Crossland stood for an appreciable time looking at the back of the man who had spoken. Then, without another word, he resumed his pacing.

"Will you do the killing, Harringay?" young Mathers asked.

"I would—if it were necessary that I should do it," said Harringay. He normally had the voice of a toastmaster, and when he lowered it in order to speak confidentially, it gave one the impression of a river rumbling over a rocky bed. "But I don't see why I should carry the whole thing through on my own back," he added. "I've suggested the method. Perhaps somebody else would prefer to carry it into execution."

Forbes put out a foot, and with the toe of his shoe delicately adjusted a piece of coal on the fire.

"After all, Crossland," he murmured, "it isn't Harringay's sister; it's your sister."

"I know that," Crossland replied impatiently, coming to a pause on the sheepskin hearthrug. "But we needn't insist on that point. We're all in the racket, whether the girl concerned happens to be my sister or not."

"Don't use the word 'racket,' old chap," Forbes begged. "Call it a something of mercy—campaign of mercy."

"Call it what you like," said Mathers, the young fellow with the smooth black hair and the thin lips. "But let's get something settled. Where is he now? Do any of you know?"

He rose from the arm of the chair and carried his glass to the sideboard, and stood there dispensing another drink.

"Go careful with that stuff," said Forbes. "Not that you aren't welcome to it, but we don't want you to be fuddled."

"He's at his digs, I suppose," Harringay rumbled, in answer to Mathers' question.

"That hole!" Mathers exclaimed, making the siphon sizzle.

"Don't know so much about 'that hole!' " said Crossland from the sheepskin hearthrug. "He's got a dam' fine laboratory at the back, anyway."

"Have you been there?" Forbes asked, looking up for the first time.

"No," said Crossland. "But Sis told me. She's been there."

"*Has* she?"

"Yes. Three times that I know of. Oftener, probably. She doesn't tell me now. She hasn't told me anything since I kicked up a shindy with her about it."

"You shouldn't have done that," Forbes commented, fingering his black bow. "You only antagonize her. It encourages her to let her infatuation run riot."

Mathers interrupted with a gesture of impatience.

"Never mind about that now," he exclaimed. "The point is that if she marries him, she can't marry me."

"The point is," said Crossland, "that if she marries him she marries a damned madman. That's what I've got to think about. After all, she *is* my sister."

The ghost of a smile touched the corners of Harringay's mouth.

"You haven't got to think about the money, I suppose?" he said.

"Well—"

"We might as well face the position squarely," Harringay continued. "It's true that Sissie Crossland is your sister, and it's true that you wouldn't like to see her tied up to anybody who's insane. But the chief thing is that if she marries him he'll take her fortune to spend on his scientific work. She'll take it out of our hands, and where will we be then? We'll be ruined—all of us."

"And jailed, I shouldn't be surprised."

It was Forbes who spoke. Forbes had returned to his contemplation of the red heart of the fire.

His comment was very apt. The four of them were gambling heavily with the fortune belonging to Crossland's sister, and though they were sure that they could eventually land themselves on velvet—as Harringay put it—they were temporarily in very shallow water—also as Harringay put it. And not only would the withdrawal of their capital at the present moment make it impossible for them to get back their losses—it might also bring them under the notice of those officials whose job it is to safeguard the gullible public, and that would be the most serious of all. Sissie Crossland had relied upon her brother to see that her money was safely invested in gilt-edged securities, for she knew nothing about financial matters; and while she received 3½ per cent interest she was satisfied. But if she were to marry, her husband would undoubtedly discover that her money was not where she thought it was; then there would be such a row and a rumpus.

Yes, Forbes' comment about being jailed was very apt.

"If we're left undisturbed for six months at the most," Harringay pointed out, "we can call ourselves safe. If we're asked before then to give an account of our—stewardship—"

He left the sentence in the air. Young Mathers glanced at him from beneath lowered eyelids, while his fingers twitched.

"I don't want to get ten years," he said. "There can't be any doubt about her marrying him, Crossland?" he asked.

"None whatever," said Crossland. "He's years older than she is, and he's insane, if ever a man was insane. But she just won't see it. I can't make any impression upon her. I don't understand it. She used to be fairly level-headed, but now she seems to have let infatuation run away with her altogether. Yet, I don't see how we can *kill* him—"

"That's twice you've said that, Crossland," Forbes pointed out. "Can you suggest any other way out of the difficulty?"

"Well—"

"You understand that if she marries him we're done for?"

"I see that—yes."

"He'll want to know where her money is."

"Probably."

"Not probably—certainly. He's living in a hole of a place, as Mathers called it. I expect that every penny he's got is being spent on his scientific work. Obviously he's hard up. Scientific research costs a lot of money. Therefore, the first thing he'll do when he marries a wealthy girl will be to induce her to part with a considerable lump of her fortune. Your sister will ask you to realize part of the investments you are supposed to have made on her behalf, and we're finished."

Forbes had turned towards the room while he was speaking. Now he leant upon the mantelpiece again, and with the toe of his shoe pressed another piece of coal down into the fire.

"And you say we can't kill him!" he murmured. "You realize what ten years in prison means, I suppose?"

Forbes was the evil genius of the gathering. He, even to a greater extent than the middle-aged Harringay, could look at the position squarely, uninfluenced by moral considerations.

The aptness of his remarks showed how clearly he had the situation in focus. And the comparative calmness of his manner hinted at the darkness and the deadliness of his thoughts.

Yes, it was Forbes who was the evil genius of the gathering. Crossland, the brother of the girl whose money had brought about the present situation, was obviously a man lacking in courage. He had been capable of cheating his sister, but now that the day of reckoning was hinted at he had not the character either to face the girl or to adopt the one terrible plan to save himself and his three companions from disaster. He knew not to expect leniency from Cynthia; the loss of between twenty and thirty thousand pounds was not a matter that even the most forgiving of sisters would accept cheerfully; and the fact of his being her brother would, in this case, have no effect on the seriousness of his plight, for she would certainly take action against Forbes and Harringay and Mathers, and he would inevitably be swept in with the rest. A long term of imprisonment was a dreadful thing to contemplate. So was a murder.

He didn't think he could commit murder. To do that, a man would have to be keyed up to an extreme pitch of desperation. He thought he would rather take the risk of a long term of imprisonment—all the nerve-racking suspense, the degrading publicity of a trial, and the long, dead years of misery, when he and other felons would be herded together in a world wherein was no hope, but only monotony that killed the soul. Yet, to lose the glorious years of a man's life between the ages of twenty-five and thirty-five . . .

He had no very strict conscience. He was not the kind of man who might die for a principle. If he were ever to risk death, it would only be because he was forced into taking the risk so that some personal disaster might be avoided. He was capable of maintaining that it was not wrong to kill, and he firmly believed that it was not wrong to kill. Only, in a way he did not understand, killing inspired a certain horror in his mind—a horror that he tried to deride, telling himself that it sprang from timidity.

"I don't see anything else for it," said Forbes, turning and looking at each of the men separately. "We can't afford to take risks. You're agreed upon that, I suppose?"

Young Mathers was breathing heavily. Despite his cruel-looking lips and the general marks of hard living that were evident in his drawn features, he was trembling.

It was to the young men—Mathers and Crossland—that Forbes addressed his enquiry. The fifty-year-old Harringay already stood committed to the extreme course that would enable them to avoid disaster. It was conceivable that Harringay had already had experience in taking extreme courses; he looked that sort of man—a man who had served his apprenticeship in a hard school, and who had long since overcome his native Puritanical inhibitions.

"And who is going to do the killing?" Mathers asked, glancing inimically at Forbes as though he thought there might be a catch somewhere.

"Yes, who's going to do the killing?" Crossland echoed.

Forbes shrugged his shoulders.

"Oh, don't think I'm trying to trick you fellows into doing more than your share of the work," he said. "Let's be quite fair about it. We're all in the boat together; we all ought to take an equal chance. Will you abide by the cut of the cards?"

Crossland looked at Mathers, then at Harringay.

"Yes," he said, bringing the word out in a staccato whisper, while his gaze shifted to Forbes.

"I'm game," said Mathers. The hard-bitten youth spoke in a shaky voice.

"Count me in," Harringay muttered negligently.

"And myself, of course," said Forbes. He wasted no time, but stepped across to a cabinet in a corner and returned with a new pack of cards.

And so the four men cut the cards, one after another, seven times round so that there might be no doubt about the fairness of the count, having agreed that he whose total was lowest should commit the murder.

Crossland, too, was trembling now. While the business was under discussion there had been a vagueness about the future, and though that had not been pleasant it had at least left room for hope that some solution might be found. But now the four were pinned down to a definite course of action, and there could be no evading that course of action. Still, there were three chances to one against his being chosen.

Three chances to one! And seven rounds of cutting! He did not know what the chances were after the first round, and he himself stood midway with a seven. Then he cut a king, which counted thirteen; then a four, followed by an ace, which counted one; then another ace; then a six.

Thirty-two, and one round to go . . .

He took out his handkerchief and wiped his forehead. The room was close. He saw the face of Forbes at the other side of the table. The face was inscrutable but for a slight twitching about one corner of the mouth. Forbes' score stood at twenty-eight. Mathers had reached forty-seven and was safe. Harringay stood at thirty-six. If Harringay should get a one, it would mean that he himself need get only something over five. For a moment he did not fully understand how the pack of cards had come into the affair at all. He could not believe that they were cutting not to decide who should deal, but to decide who should commit a murder. It couldn't be true. Yet, it was true.

It was the heat of the room that was making his senses dull so that he seemed to be in the midst of a nightmare.

Harringay cut an ace. You could hear Harringay breathing. Forbes cut a nine and stood for a moment staring at it as though he saw his doom written across the face of the card. Forbes and Harringay were thirty-seven each. Crossland, with one cut in hand, stood at thirty-two. The cards had been coming up in small numbers. While Mathers shuffled the pack, Crossland tried to work out the odds in his own favour. Anything over five would save him, and there were eight cards over five and only four below. Two chances to one. And low numbers had predominated. Did that affect the odds in favour of a high number this time?

His thoughts went misty. The cards were lying on the table. The room was unbearably hot. He put out his hand weakly and picked up a third of the pack. The three of diamonds stared up at him.

He laughed. He did not mean to laugh. He did not know why he laughed.

"A close thing!" he said.

Harringay handed him a glass of whisky.

"We'll help you, of course," said Forbes.

"That's all right," he replied. "I shan't want any help. It will be easier without help. One can slip away, where four might be caught. And, anyway, I have a personal interest in the man. I'm convinced that he's insane. And my sister is going to marry him. It is my duty to put him out of the way."

Presently the gathering broke up.

Harringay, Mathers and Crossland descended to the pavement of Regent Street, emerging by a door situated between two shops. Harringay was holding Crossland by the arm, above the elbow, and from time to time he glanced at him surreptitiously, and carried the glance beyond him to Mathers. Mathers, however, was in as great a state of nervousness as Crossland.

"All right, old man," said Crossland with a touch of impatience, disengaging Harringay's hand. "I can manage quite well. I'm not upset about it. No need for me to be upset. If your sister was going to marry an insane scientist—or insane anything—wouldn't you consider it your duty to—"

"Ssh!" said Harringay warningly. "Don't talk so loudly, old

chap . . . But I certainly should. Especially as it saves the lot of us from prison."

"Never mind about that," Crossland took him up, speaking with the excessive assertiveness of one who is drunk. "What did Forbes call it? . . . Campaign of mercy! That was it—campaign of mercy! And that's how I look at it. As for you, Mathers," he went on somewhat pugnaciously, "what would you have done had you cut lowest? Shall I tell you what you would have done? You would have called the deal off. That's what you would have done."

Harringay swore under his breath, then glanced meaningly at Mathers and frowned.

"Well, good night, gentlemen," said Mathers, taking the hint and pretending not to have heard Crossland.

He turned up the collar of his coat and drifted off as gracefully as he could into the pedestrian stream, and was soon lost among the quickly-changing lights and shadows.

Crossland watched him go, then he turned to Harringay.

"Lucky for you that he wasn't picked," he said. "He's all 'nerves' as it is. He seems to think it's murder, and the very thought of it has sent him groggy. But it isn't murder. It's saving my sister from a life of horror—that's what it is."

"That's right, old boy!" Harringay spoke enthusiastically, laying his hand on the young man's shoulder as an earnest of his complete agreement. "Keep hold of that idea, and you'll carry it through fine."

"Don't you believe me?"

"Believe you?"

"Yes. When I say that he's a man who ought to be—made to vanish!"

"Why, of course I believe you."

"I don't know whether you do, Harringay. I don't know whether you can. You might if you knew my sister at all well. But you don't know her and you can't judge. You can take it from me, however, that there's something not right about that fellow she's fallen for. There's something *unholy* about him. Afraid I can't explain just what I mean."

Harringay concluded that the young man was drunk, that the cold, fresh air had sent the whisky fumes to his head. He offered to see him home, but Crossland would have none of it.

And when Crossland eventually walked off in a northerly direction he walked steadily enough.

CHAPTER II

CYNTHIA

CYNTHIA CROSSLAND was afraid. At moments her fear amounted to terror, and it was not the less real because she did not know whence it sprang.

The feeling had been growing upon her during the past month. She could not tell when first she became aware of it—that feeling of uneasiness to begin with, gradually becoming more and more noticeable.

She thought she was run-down and wanted a tonic, although she was not the sort to be in need of tonics. And she could not really believe that she was run-down. She was just afraid of something—she could not tell what. And if this was a case of nerves being out of order, then nerves were funny things and she didn't want to have any more of them.

In fact, if one thought about nerves and the way in which they seemed to be able to affect one's outlook, there was no saying where the thought would lead. She knew that people could drive themselves mad if they thought hard enough about it. It just wanted a touch to set you going on the road towards nervousness, and once you were started you did not seem to be able to stop. And the world was such an immense place, and there were so many tremendous forces in it, that a mere individual hardly seemed to have a chance of survival, to say nothing of a chance of happiness.

She wondered whether she ought to go away for a holiday. The doctor had said there was nothing whatever the matter with her. However, she would go abroad for a month or two. It would give her a change of scenery and a change of interest. It would also, perhaps, break her of her strange infatuation for Michel Benni.

She was reclining on a chesterfield in the room that she was pleased to call a study. It was a comparatively small room when taken in conjunction with the rest of the house, which was immense. Of the Crossland family there remained only Cynthia herself and her brother Harold, and they lived in this big house on the edge of Regent's Park because the house had always been their home, and because it had been left to them by their mother, a couple of years earlier.

Harold had suggested letting it and going into a flat, but Cynthia had not been eager to hand her old home over to the care of strangers. And Harold had not been able to enforce his own will upon her because he relied on her to keep him supplied with money. They had both been left a comparatively small sum by their parents, but Harold had quickly run through his. She assumed that it was natural for a man to do so, although she couldn't see the wisdom of it. For herself, she had had a considerable slice of luck when an uncle she had never seen had made her his sole heir, so she felt that it was her duty to keep Harold supplied with money.

She had much more than she required, and she did not mind spending her income up to the last farthing. Her investments were as safe as they could be, and they yielded well over a thousand a year. She had resisted the temptation to have a shot at speculating. Harold had been all for it, pointing out the folly of investing money in return for a thousand a year when she might, with reasonable safety, get four thousand. She had replied by pointing out the folly of taking any risk whatsoever when gilt-edged investments gave her quite as much money as she wanted.

And Harold, having no legal say in the matter, was forced to agree with her.

No, she wasn't going to be browbeaten into taking unnecessary risks. She didn't know much about finance, she admitted, but she knew enough not to play fast and loose with what represented her staple income. And the fact that Harold knew quite a lot about finance did not induce her to be influenced by his advice; she instructed him to buy the stocks she knew were perfectly sound, and that was that.

She wondered whether she ought to shut the house up, or let it, as Harold had suggested, and go into a flat. She knew she would feel dreadfully cramped in a flat after having had the run of this big house and garden for the whole of her twenty-two years.

On the other hand, perhaps the bigness of the house, and the fact that it stood solitary in its own grounds, had helped to induce the curious nervousness from which she was now suffering.

At the moment, for instance, she was in the place alone but for the two elderly servants who had been retained. These two had retired for the night, and were now far up at the top of the house. Many dark, unused rooms lay between them and herself, for the study was on the ground level. It was at the side of the house, and looked out on to a stretch of lawn that was backed by a thick mass of rhododendron, and it was called a study simply because it had always been called a study, although it was now more of a boudoir than anything else.

She was waiting for Harold to come home and was trying to occupy herself with a novel. But the novel would not grip. The fault lay with herself; her mind would wander away to other things. Harold's propensity for keeping late hours was a matter that did not add to her peace of mind. He was three years older than she, but she felt herself to be in the position of guardian towards him. She was not *very* proud of him. He had not the strength of character that she wanted him to have. They sometimes quarrelled, he and she, and then she would let him know what she thought of him and would give it as her opinion that a little hard contact with the world would do him good. And she meant it. Harold was the kind of man who would unquestionably benefit from some bitter experience . . . Then there was Michel Benni.

Her thoughts broke off short, and she sat up in alarm.

The alarm, however, was caused by nothing more than the sharp ringing of the telephone bell. The instrument was over in a corner of the room, and its sudden awakening to life was certainly startling, but it was not like Cynthia to be startled by an ordinary sound whose cause was plainly apparent, and that she now sat for some seconds staring at the instrument without making any attempt to rise and walk towards it was a very clear proof of the state of her nerves. She did not know what she feared, but she had a conviction, not born of reason, that disaster of some sort was imminent, and she saw in every innocent event the warning of doom. An unexpected invitation to dinner, the chance meeting with a stranger, the ringing of the telephone bell—events of that sort frightened her. Especially the ringing of the telephone bell.

But it was all right. The caller was only Eddie Landor. Eddie was a very persistent young man, she reflected, when she recognized his voice, hut she could wish that his persistence would not carry him to the length of ringing her up at close on midnight.

"I might have turned in for the night," she pointed out, when she had remonstrated with him for the untimeliness of his call. "And you know how insistent and irresistible a telephone bell is. It would certainly have wakened me and I should have had to come down all those stairs—because, you know, you can't just turn over and go to sleep again. And, anyway, what do you want?"

"First of all," said the caller, "I want to tell you that I knew you hadn't turned in for the night. I passed your place in my car less than a minute ago. I saw your light burning—in that little den of yours, you know—and I thought that here was a good chance."

"A good chance of what?"

"A good chance of asking you something."

"Yes. Go on. I'm listening."

"Will you marry me?"

"Will I—"

"Marry me!"

"But I say, Eddie!"

"Will you?"

"You have asked me that before, you know."

"I know I have—each time with more and more hope."

"And I've told you—"

"You have told me that you couldn't think of it—each time with less and less assurance. If I ask often enough, there will come a time when your assurance will have vanished completely. And that will be equivalent to an acceptance."

"I'm afraid not, Eddie. I like you immensely—"

"Right-ho, dear! No need to try to soften the blow. For it isn't a blow, really; you are only deferring the happy day. You will eventually say you'll marry me, won't you?"

"But, Eddie, haven't I told you—"

"Quite, quite! But you see, dear, I'm so frightfully keen about you . . . And I might say I was rather hopeful this time. I hear that there isn't anything between you and Charlie Mathers, after all. Everybody thought there was."

"Perhaps there was. But the truth is that I don't want to get married."

"Not even to me?"

"Not even to you, Eddie . . ."

There was a pause lasting, perhaps, five seconds. And in that pause the emotional atmosphere changed. So far the exchange of remarks had been on the plane of the facetious, almost; but with Cynthia's last words there had been introduced a trembling intensity that Eddie detected.

"Cynthia," he said, and his voice dropped a tone or two down to the resonant bass of a man who is quietly serious, "what's the matter?"

"Nothing's the matter," she assured him, speaking lightly.

"I'm coming round to see you," he said then.

"To see me? . . . But you can't—you mustn't. Think of the time. Don't be so silly, Eddie."

"You're alone, I suppose? Harold isn't there, is he?"

"No; I'm waiting up for him. But, Eddie—"

"That's all right then. Harold won't mind my calling at your place even at midnight, so I'll be along in just about half a minute. You see, I'm in the telephone kiosk at the corner of the road."

"But you mustn't call at this time of night, Eddie."

He could hear the note of alarm in her voice, but he knew that the alarm was not due to fears regarding the propriety of his call. It was due to something else—something of which he had only the faintest inkling, but which had been causing him quite a lot of concern lately. There was something troubling Cynthia, and he meant to find out what it was.

CHAPTER III

MICHEL BENNI

EDDIE LANDOR, as he stepped out of the telephone kiosk and slipped into the driving-seat of his car, wondered whether he was not exceeding the bounds even of very good friendship in thus forcing himself upon Cynthia at this hour of the night. His only justification was the conviction that there was something wrong with her, and he could risk her displeasure for the sake of the chance of doing her a service.

He did not see her very often, but he saw her often enough to notice that lately she had grown very unlike her usual self, and Harold, her brother, had told him that she had formed an odd friendship with a curious individual—a chemist or a doctor or something—who lived in one room in a Bloomsbury back street, and who was a foreigner and reputed to be mad.

Now Eddie knew Cynthia Crossland to be, above all things, a perfectly level-headed young person in normal circumstances, and although it was conceivable that she might on occasion do something out of the ordinary—something even fantastic—it would only be by way of a lark, one would imagine, and would have neither profound significance nor distressing consequences. But here was something that seemed to have both; even Harold was worried about it, and Harold was not a man to worry himself unnecessarily about other people's affairs. Harold, in fact, had gone so far as to say that she was going to marry this crazy foreign scientist, but that, of course, could not be true.

Eddie ran his car into the dark drive that fronted the Crosslands' house, then felt his way up the dark steps and gave the bell just the merest touch.

The hall was only dimly lighted, apparently from the open door of the study. Cynthia, wishing to keep this midnight visit as secret as possible, had no doubt opened the door slightly so that she would hear the bell. And with the same object of secrecy, she had not switched on either the hall light or the opal globe under the portico.

She did not immediately answer his ring, however. He guessed that she was hesitating in indecision about the propriety of opening the door. Or perhaps, by now, she had made up her mind not to open the door—to teach him not to presume too much upon the friendship that existed between them. After all, it was a bit of cheek on his part to expect her to see him at this time of night on business that had really nothing to do with him. He had acted upon impulse; happening to pass the house and happening to see the light in the study window, he had thought it would be quite a good wheeze to ring her from the first telephone kiosk and ask her to marry him. He frequently asked her to marry him, and because of the frequency of his proposals they had to be made facetiously, even though he might be in deadly earnest, and this midnight telephone call had been quite in keeping with his general behaviour. But he had not intended to pay a visit to the house. It was her tone—the tone that hinted at dark mystery—that had made him suddenly decide to have a serious talk with her in the hope of gaining her confidence and so finding out what was wrong.

It did not seem, however, as if she intended to let him have that opportunity.

He was about to ring the bell again when he realized, with a start, that he was not alone under the dark portico. Another man stood there—a still, silent being, hardly discernible in the black, diffused shadows cast by the massive pillars.

"Well, you're a rum customer," Eddie reflected, quickly recovering from his surprise and surreptitiously studying the individual who stood in the shadows.

At the first instant of being aware of the other man's presence he had thought that here was someone hanging about the place with some felonious intention, but a second glance showed that he was apparently mistaken. The man had the appearance of a gentleman, in dress and carriage, as far as the darkness permitted these points to be noticed; and in any case, he did not try to slink away as he might have done had he been a criminal surprised in attempting to force the lock of the front door. On the contrary, he stood there very fixedly—even aggressively, Eddie thought—not in the least disconcerted by the appearance of a second caller.

The only suspicious feature of his presence was the fact of his keeping right within the shadows cast by the pillars. It seemed odd that he should stand so far to one side of the door, and in the deepest gloom, when there was plenty of space on the tessellated square directly in front of the door.

"I understand there is somebody at home," Eddie ventured to remark, by way of easing the strange tension of the moment.

It struck him that this might be a doctor and that one of the two old servants was ill. The man certainly had the air of a doctor—that air of quiet restraint that generally marks the professional man.

Be that as it may, he did not hazard any answer to Eddie's remark, but continued to stand very quiet and still in the shadows.

"You *are* a rum customer," Eddie reflected, feeling the slightest bit confused by the man's steady stare. But he realized that there might be many explanations of the fellow's conduct. He might be deaf, for one thing, and that might account both for his silence and for his stepping well aside so that he should not be drawn into conversation.

Eddie was not reassured, however, by that possible explanation of the man's silence, and he felt decidedly uneasy under the stare that was being directed at him.

"Mad, maybe," he thought, and putting out his hand, he gave the bell-push another light touch.

Presently the glow within the hall was broken by a moving shadow, then the hall lights were switched on and the big front door was noiselessly opened.

Cynthia had no smile for him as she stepped back, opening the door wide. She had on a pale green dress, and her very fair hair was arranged with its accustomed neatness, but these attractive features of her appearance were not supported by the usual sparkle of her eyes. She seemed distressed, and Eddie thought that he had done well to make this unorthodox call, for she could not very well maintain that there was nothing the matter.

He was about to step over the threshold when he remembered that the other man, having called first, should take precedence. He stepped aside, and was about to incline his head as an indication to the other fellow to go in first, when he discovered that the man had moved away from his position in the shadows of the pillars and that, in fact, he was now nowhere to be seen.

"Somebody else was waiting here when I arrived," he explained to Cynthia. "But he seems to have gone."

He looked more closely among the pillars and gazed down the short drive which was now partly illuminated by the light from the hall, but there was neither sight nor sound of the strange being who had stood still and silent among the shadows.

"That's very queer," Eddie murmured. "He must have slipped away."

He stepped into the hall on Cynthia's wordless invitation, and closed the door after him. Cynthia had made no comment on the stranger mentioned as having been waiting. That is to say, she made no spoken comment. But her manner was a comment, for she looked uneasy to the extent of appearing definitely afraid; and in a flash Eddie realized—or, at least, guessed—that the man in the shadows had been the person spoken of by Harold, Cynthia's brother.

Harold had said that the fellow was mad—a crazy scientist or something. And if the fellow made a habit of standing in dark corners and neither answering nor moving when he was spoken to, it was little wonder that he was considered to be not quite the thing mentally.

"What do you want to see me about?" Cynthia asked, as she turned and led the way towards the study.

"About that man who was waiting outside," Eddie answered, glancing at her to see how she would react to his words. He only hoped she would not ask him to leave, as she might very well do if he should take too much upon himself. It was all very well to ask her at every opportunity when she was going to marry him, but he realized that if he were to exceed the bounds of ordinary friendship and begin interfering with her private life, she might be very ruthless in her treatment of him.

She frowned. Rather, a look that was half a frown and half an expression of pain crossed her features. It was obvious that she did not welcome the reference to the man who had been standing in the shadows outside, but at least she did not openly resent the reference.

Eddie, as he followed her into the study, noted one point in her behaviour that was to puzzle him for quite a long time. That is to say, she expressed neither surprise nor curiosity respecting the person who was the subject of Eddie's remark. She did not question Eddie about him, nor had she seemed at all concerned on learning that someone had been standing on the doorstep and had then mysteriously gone. It was as though it were customary for silent, motionless men to stand in the shadows about the house; one took no notice of them, regarding their presence and their sudden disappearance as being quite in the ordinary nature of human behaviour, and not worthy of being enquired into.

"You aren't going to ask me to marry you?" she said, as she resumed her seat on the chesterfield, leaving him, such was the familiar nature of their friendship, to find a chair for himself.

"Well, not at the moment," he replied. "Seeing you refused me less than five minutes ago, I can hardly expect you to have altered your mind already. Even *my* optimism does not rise to that height."

"Five minutes ago?" she asked.

"Not more, surely," he said, and looked at her strangely.

Judging by her tone, one would say that she did not remember the proposal of less than five minutes ago.

"You mean when you telephoned to me?" she asked.

"Yes," he told her. "I telephoned from the box along at the corner."

"So you said when you rang," she remarked. "You also said you would be along in less than a minute—or less than half a minute, was it?"

"Less than half a minute, I think I said," he replied. "I was perhaps cutting it too fine, however."

She smiled, meanwhile shaking her head slowly as she looked into his eyes. Her manner was that of one who was moved by indulgent pity for another's shortcomings.

"But, my dear boy," she said, "that was over an hour ago. I like your idea of time! Where did you get to? Did you lose your way?"

Eddie tried hard not to look puzzled, but he was thinking, "My dear Cynthia, are you mad or am I?"

"Over an hour ago?" he echoed.

Control was difficult, but he felt that he was acting in a manner that would not cause her alarm. He knew without question that not more than one minute had elapsed between the time of his leaving the telephone box and the time of his pressing the bell at the front door of this house. And thereafter perhaps two minutes had elapsed—certainly not more than two minutes—before he pressed the bell for the second time and was admitted.

A strange kind of fear took hold of him. He felt that he had come to the knowledge of matters buried deep in the abyss of the human mind—matters beyond clear conception, mysterious matters hinting at awful forces working in those deeps, so that what was to one mind two minutes was to another mind a full hour.

Here, he was convinced, was some indication of whatever might be amiss with Cynthia, although he could not grasp its significance. Cynthia imagined, quite honestly and without the faintest doubt to make her uneasy, that over an hour had passed during the few minutes that had just gone. She might have slept, of course; but she did not look as though she had been asleep, and she would assuredly know if she had been asleep. But perhaps not. Sleep, he reflected, was a curious thing—in some ways more mysterious than death itself.

"Perhaps you are right," he said, glancing at the clock on the mantelpiece. The clock was correct to within a few minutes, as he discovered when he compared it with his watch, and showed a minute or two after midnight.

"It must have been before eleven when you telephoned," she said. "What have you been doing since?"

"I ran into an old friend of mine," he lied, grateful for a convenient turn of invention. "I stopped to exchange a few words with him, and I suppose didn't notice how the time was flying. I trust you will forgive me."

"It wasn't very chivalrous of you, was it?" she teased him, without any pouting coquettishness, but as though she might be his fond sister.

"No," he admitted. "And I'm extremely sorry. Did the time hang heavily on your hands?"

He tried to keep his voice normal as he asked this, but he was well aware that here was an opportunity for discovering something that might be of help to him in finding out what was the matter with this girl. Thinking of the lively enthusiasm that had been hers up to a few months ago, and noting her present absence of high spirits and her general strangeness, and viewing the whole in conjunction with Harold's story of her infatuation for a mad scientist, Eddie had been wondering whether the trouble might be merely a kind of nervous breakdown or whether the mad scientist had anything to do with it. And now he reflected that it might be worth a lot to know what her experiences had been during those two min utes that had seemed to her like something over an hour.

"No," she assured him; "the time did not hang heavily on my hands. In point of fact, a friend called just a few minutes after you telephoned, and he and I sat here talking."

"A friend?"

"Yes," she said. "I don't mind telling you, Eddie, for you can't think it wrong of me to allow a man friend to call on me so late at night when you call even later."

"Oh, I shouldn't dream of thinking it wrong of you," he stated. "I know you well enough for that. But I'm frightfully jealous all the same."

When he said that, a look of uneasiness crossed her face. He did not think it presumptuous of himself to believe that she had a certain affection for him. He could even imagine that he might have induced her to marry him had he put himself forward earlier as a candidate for her favours, but he had understood that there was an understanding between her and Charlie Mathers. Mathers, however, seemed to have gone to the bad within the past year or so—taking Cynthia's brother with him—and, lately, Eddie had thought it quite in order that he himself should put in a word in his own favour.

But now another influence seemed to be guiding her choice, and he wondered whether she really did not think enough of him to take him seriously, or whether this other influence was actually forcing her to go against her instincts. It was all very curious and profoundly disturbing. But that look of uneasiness that had crossed her face when he said he was jealous—that gave him hope. It showed that she did consider him; possibly it hinted that she was not too sure of the wisdom of her friendship with this other fellow—this reputedly crazy scientist.

"I didn't invite him here—to-night," she said, speaking as it were in self-defence. "The friend who called, I mean. I didn't know he was coming. He just arrived. I don't think I should have let him come in, but he came in. Somebody must have left the front door open, I think, and he just wandered in. A curious thing to do. He came right into this room."

"You are speaking about—"

"About Michel Benni," she said. "Yes—Michel Benni."

"Probably Harold has told you about him."

"He has mentioned him—yes. I recognize the name now that you repeat it."

"And what do you think?"

"What do I think? . . . I can hardly take it upon myself to have any thoughts upon the matter—any critical views, I mean."

"But you have, nevertheless."

"Why do you say that?"

She had been sitting gazing at the carpet. Now she raised her eyes and looked straight at Eddie.

"I can't but think that Harold has been trying to influence you against Michel Benni," she said. "And you have naturally paid some attention to Harold. Isn't that true?"

"Well—"

"I ask you if that isn't true," she insisted, with a sudden show of heat. "Hasn't Harold told you that Michel Benni is mad? Hasn't he told you that?"

Eddie tried to pacify her by himself remaining calm.

"Well," he said, "I have certainly got the impression that this Michel Benni is a little unusual. Harold is surprised at your choice."

"And you take notice of Harold's opinion," she said quietly, giving Eddie a look, nevertheless, that made him feel as though he had acted disloyally towards her. "Harold is quite an uninspired person," she went on. "To Harold, life has nothing to offer more elevating than a jazz band in a night club. That is Harold. He isn't capable of appreciating a man like Michel Benni."

"Pleased don't be annoyed with me," Eddie protested. "I'm not Harold. I'm prepared to believe that Michel Benni is a very great man."

"A very great man," she echoed. "Yes, that is it—a very great man."

"I accept your estimate," he said. "I might have known that this Michel Benni was someone out of the ordinary to have claimed your affections."

"As for that," she replied hesitatingly, "I don't think I said that he had claimed my affections. That isn't quite the term to use in connection with Michel Benni."

Eddie felt that he was beginning to see light, albeit the light tended to confuse rather than to clarify. Cynthia seemed to be infatuated with the man, who had apparently impressed her with his greatness, so one could hope that the state of infatuation would pass. On the other hand there was something very disturbing in her having imagined that a long time had passed during the two minutes following the telephone call.

One might assume that the cause of this was some form of amnesia or forgetfulness of an abnormal character, and that the blank period had been filled in with imaginary happenings that had seemed to take a long time for their enacting. Such a condition, Eddie reflected, might occur in the case of a person suffering from even only a slight disturbance of the nervous system, and it was not necessarily a matter about which to worry. And he would not have worried had it not been for the other features of the case, particularly the strange presence of the man who had stood silently in the shadows under the portico.

That presence had something sinister about it, and Eddie wondered whether the man, standing outside the house, had been able to influence the mental processes of Cynthia, who had been inside the house.

"You mean that Michel Benni is beyond such trivial feelings as mere affection?" he asked, with the object of inducing her to explain herself more fully.

"I can hardly say what his feelings are," she said. "I can only say what kind of feeling he inspires in others. I don't know whether you would call it affection. I think it might more readily be called fear."

"Fear?" Eddie echoed. She smiled faintly.

"I don't know whether you can understand," she said, "you being a man. Ordinary love is a sufficiently terrifying thing to a girl. Even where there is complete understanding between her and a man, there is always a certain fear. And Michel Benni is not the kind of man of whom one can have complete understanding. There is something tremendously powerful about him. He compels affection, admiration, hero-worship—call it what you like. He is the most wonderful man I have ever met. He frightens me. I feel that in making a friend of him, I am putting myself in the way of incalculable experiences, terrifying experiences. But I can't help it. There must be a streak of morbidity in me that makes me court danger for its own sake. I don't know. Sometimes I want to run away. I thought of going for a holiday; only this evening I was thinking of that. Then he arrived—as I told you—and I felt that I was merely being silly. I'm not afraid of him really; only there are some intellects so vastly superior to one's own that one feels utterly insignificant. And, feeling insignificant, one cannot but be afraid of circumstances. Yet, there is something delicious in the feeling . . . He asked me to marry him—when he was here just now, before you arrived. I said I would. Harold thinks he's mad; but he is anything but mad. I don't know why I am telling you all this, Eddie. I think it must be because I have a very great regard for you."

Her voice had sunk almost to a whisper while she was making these remarks. Eddie could not but notice her growing emotion, but he chose to disregard it. And he was careful not to tell her that she had imagined the hour's visit of Michel Benni. If she were to know that she could not trust her own observation, the effect upon her nervous and mental states would be very serious indeed.

"That was Michel Benni who left as I arrived?" he asked.

"Yes," she said. "I didn't go to the door with him. He let himself out. Then you rang, almost at once."

"And you answered my ring—promptly," Eddie said, making of the words a remark and not a question, but waiting anxiously for her comment.

"Yes," she said, "of course."

This was more alarming than ever. It would seem that the hour's visit that she had lived through in imagination had occurred, if such a term is permissible, during the few moments between Eddie's two rings at the bell.

Further enquiry into the matter was for the moment suspended, however, by the arrival of Harold.

Eddie wondered whether he ought to tell Harold about the night's mysterious phenomena, but decided not to do so yet. For one thing, Harold did not seem to be in the happiest state for considering matters of that sort. Eddie had a suspicion that Harold had been drinking, and, after a few formal words, he took his leave.

He formed a decision to meet this Michel Benni in order to see just what the man was really like.

CHAPTER IV

GURLITT ROW

ON the following evening, at dusk, Harold Crossland let himself out of the house and slunk down the short drive and out on to the pavement. He did not wish to be observed by Cynthia or by either of the two maids, for he was not dressed as he usually was in the evenings, but wore a very old overcoat, the collar of which was turned up, and a soft felt hat with a dipping brim.

Despite the fact that he had not yet offended against the law he already felt guilty, but presently he braced his shoulders, telling himself that even when he should have despatched Michel Benni he would not have committed murder.

He had had a long talk with Cynthia on the previous night. She had been in an amiable mood, and he had made a last endeavour to influence her against Michel Benni, but he quickly realized that she was not to be influenced. More, he was confirmed in his suspicions that his sister's association with Michel Benni was certainly preying on her mind. Only one who knew Cynthia well could realize to what extent she had altered during the past few months, and Harold took courage from that fact as he set out towards Bloomsbury.

In the pocket of his overcoat he had a revolver. He felt that he could not kill by any other means, unless it might be with his bare fists; and he had to confess that he was not too confident of being able to despatch Michel Benni with bare fists. The man was very powerfully built, and any advantage that Harold might have in youthful agility would be of little use to him in a hand-to-hand grapple where the deciding factor must be weight and sheer brute strength. And Harold could not forget that the man was insane; he had already assured himself of that simply by speaking to him on two or three occasions, and it amazed him to find that Cynthia was blind to that feature.

But Harold, intent on destroying the man who would assuredly destroy Cynthia if matters were left to go their own way, viewed the man's insanity in conjunction with the present expedition, and had already decided that no mistake must be made and no risk taken. Shooting was not the most honourable method of killing, but it was the most certain—and it was the least nauseating. There was something to be said for the use of a knife, but only one thing—namely, that it was silent. And there was something to be said for the use of poison, the chief merit of poison being that it could be administered without being attended by the circumstances of violence; to kill by means of poison was as easy as handing someone a cup of coffee. But there were possible delays and difficulties in the way of poisoning, and Harold Crossland's nervous state could not brook delays and difficulties.

As he walked towards Bloomsbury, he kept himself keyed up to the necessary pitch of determination. He thought, incidentally, about the money that he and his three friends had misappropriated—the money belonging to Cynthia. Was the life of a madman of more value than ten years taken from the lives of four sane persons? And was the life of a madman to be bought at the expense of one's sister's happiness?

What was it that Forbes had called it? A campaign of mercy!

He must stick to that thought. Despite his reasoned conviction that he was doing right in removing Michel Benni his inhibitions, ignoring reasoning, told him that he was doing wrong. Hundreds of years of moral training named homicide a sin, and it was all but impossible for him to think of it as being other than a sin. He could reason that before the Decalogue was given to Britain, Britons killed each other and thought nothing of it, unless it might be pleasurably. Only civilization had made killing a crime and, what was more dreadful, a sin. The priests had taught the lie that to kill was to lose one's soul, to put oneself beyond redemption. The creed of the superstitious, not supported by any observed facts! A sin against Nature itself, they called it. But not so great a sin against Nature as over-eating, for example. Not a sin against Nature at all, in fact, for there was no inevitable punishment.

To argue further—which Harold had to do in order to maintain his full determination—it was civilization and not the individual man that was at fault, for civilization forbade deliberate homicide and thus thwarted the natural instinct of man, which was to destroy his enemies. And it was a sin to deny reasonable expression to the instincts; it was a sin that was followed by inevitable punishment in the shape of warped natures. Professor Freud had discovered that truth.

No, murder could be no more than an offence against the laws framed for the convenience of society and an offence, of course, against the friends of the person murdered. But in the case of Michel Benni these conditions did not operate, for Michel Benni was not a man whom society could desire to protect, and, according to Cynthia, he had no friends and had no wish to have friends, with the exception of Cynthia herself. He was a scientist, first and foremost, and was therefore a brain without a heart. There was not necessarily anything human about him, and that was true, as Harold believed, almost in the literal sense. You felt this when you were in his presence. You felt that he was an intelligence and nothing more that was of any account—a being whose mind was abnormally developed in one direction only, so that he was a madman, a monster. For insanity did not necessarily imply underdevelopment of the mental faculties; it might as readily imply over-development. A mind that was overdeveloped could not be expected to fall into line with normal thought standards, and would imagine itself to be above the laws that governed society at large. And a mind that was overdeveloped in one direction only would be even more dangerous in its potentialities, for its judgment would be utterly twisted, and its possessor would assuredly be a monomaniac with all a monomaniac's disarming sanity as to nine-tenths of his behaviour, concealing the fearsome one-tenth.

Harold had reached Tottenham Court Road by this time in his walk to Bloomsbury. He might have ridden, but his state was such that the exertion of walking seemed desirable. He was too impatient to ride. It was a curious feature of his emotional state that he felt he would not be able to sit still and bear the tedium of a short taxi journey; a longish walk would not so insistently convey the impression of laggardly movement.

Tottenham Court Road had always suggested to him all that was worst in London. This was a purely individual impression, and was probably unjustified and almost certainly slanderous. But here the good and the bad seemed to mingle without discrimination; within a stone's-throw stood the world's greatest treasure-house of knowledge, with all its benevolent influence, and within a stone's-throw were also the lowest haunts of iniquity.

He was going to commit a murder. Reason as he might, he could not reason that fact away. He was going to kill a man in cold blood. He did not reckon on there, being any quarrel, any struggle, any violent action that might give him the excuse of self-defence for what he was about to do. He would confront Michel Benni and, without explanation, would shoot him dead.

He turned off Tottenham Court Road and threaded his way eastwards through streets and squares that had been fashionable in more spacious days, past medical institutions, the registered offices of charitable societies, the dens of solicitors, and the places of business of a multitude of odd concerns, also many boarding houses calling themselves hotels.

Night had now fallen completely, and the distances were obscured rather than illuminated by the municipal lamps. In these darkened squares and side-streets pedestrians were few and their movements seemed furtive. Only in the distant traffic thoroughfares was there an occasional glimpse of the teeming life of London.

Presently he came to Gurlitt Row, a narrow street of small houses that were grimy with age. A group of ragged children played round a lamp-post. They took no notice of the man who passed them with his face hidden by the upturned collar of his coat.

The place in which Michel Benni lived was in darkness, but Harold had gathered from Cynthia that the man would be at home that evening. He rang the bell that was labelled "M. Benni" and waited, hoping that no one else in the house would answer the ring. And while he waited, glancing this way and that along Gurlitt Row with its drab squalor and its children playing about the lamp-post, he could not but think of the incongruity between this and Cynthia, who was so fastidious in her tastes. Had Michel Benni been a young man, a young student romantically poor and with all the world in front of him, the case would have been vastly different; but he was elderly and had none of the romantic attractiveness of youth such as might readily induce Cynthia to ignore the convention of social status. So his attractiveness must lie in some other direction, as Harold reminded himself for the thousandth time.

The door opened silently, without a light having been shown to warn Harold that his ring had been noticed. Michel Benni stood in the darkness of the narrow passage.

"Come in," he said, showing no surprise at seeing who the visitor was. It was just as though the fellow had been expecting him, Harold thought, and the thought was very disturbing.

Nevertheless, he followed along the passage, which he now found to be dimly lit from a room at the back. He had automatically put his right hand into the pocket of his overcoat, as much to assure himself of the presence of his revolver as to be ready to use the weapon without delay. He might have taken it out there and then and shot Michel Benni without further ceremony, but he had to be careful regarding the consequences as they might affect himself. A shot in that part of the house would undoubtedly attract attention, and Harold, besides being pledged to kill this man, wished to take every precaution for his own safety.

The laboratory was the place that he had decided upon for the murder. In the laboratory, various sounds of an unusual nature occurred from time to time, and naturally people took little notice of them; and in any case the place was in the form of a shed and was not actually connected with the house, so that a pistol shot sounding in the neighbourhood would not inevitably be traced to there, but would more likely be mistaken for a bursting tyre or a backfiring engine.

CHAPTER V

Assassination

Michel Benni did not speak as he led Harold through the bed-sitting-room that he rented. The absence of any curiosity on his part was becoming more and more alarming. It was as though he already knew why Harold had come.

He opened a door at the back of the sitting-room and stepped out into a yard, crossed the yard, and entered the laboratory; and when Harold, too, had entered he closed the door.

"You want to see me about your sister?" he then asked.

"Yes," said Harold.

He had not intended to enter into conversation with the man, but somewhere outside there was a woman calling a cat, and Harold thought it would be inadvisable to shoot while someone was so near at hand. But when the woman should go indoors, he would not delay an instant.

"Your sister has told you that she intends to marry me?" Michel Benni then asked.

"Yes," said Harold.

"And you wish to prevent the marriage?"

"Yes."

"How do you propose to prevent it?"

"I needn't tell you that," Harold said.

"No, you needn't tell me that."

Michel Benni's dark eyes glowed with something that resembled a smile, and Harold Crossland started. Could it be that Michel Benni guessed at the specific object of this visit? Could it be, indeed, that he *knew?* A multitude of fears gripped the younger man's heart. To reason that this madman could not know the object of the visit did not induce any comforting thoughts in Harold Crossland's mind. As always, when in his company, he felt that there were strange forces in the world of which he knew nothing, except that they were sinister. And at this moment he was prepared to believe that Michel Benni had the power of reading the thoughts of others, of looking into the minds of others and learning all their intentions more clearly and more surely than if they were set forth in words.

And in that case the man would certainly be aware of the intention to kill him, for it might be reasoned—assuming mind-reading as a scientific fact—that one's most persistent and most urgent thoughts would be the ones most readily yielding to outside influence.

But, be that as it might, the man was taking no steps to safeguard himself. Harold had only to draw his revolver from his pocket and fire.

If only the woman outside would find her cat and take it and herself indoors! She was in the yard next door, and a revolver shot would certainly startle her and impress itself upon her mind and she would, without doubt, be able to tell that it came from the laboratory. Harold realized that he would have to take some risk on this night, but he could not take such an extreme risk as that of shooting a man dead almost in the presence of a person so fully on the alert as she next door.

He must stay his hand for a moment or two longer.

Meanwhile, Michel Benni's dark eyes glowed with that same hint of a smile.

"You and I are at war—is it not so?" he asked, and his eyes narrowed as he spoke. Then he gave his attention to a small gas-ring that was burning under an iron vessel on the long marble slab that occupied one side of the laboratory and that was, to Harold's unskilled sight, a confusion of bottles and jars and strange instruments.

And the woman outside was still calling her cat, whose name was Teeny.

"I object to my sister marrying you," Harold replied. "I don't know whether you would call that war."

"But certainly I call that war," Michel Benni answered, looking up from the gas-ring, while his body still remained in a stooping position, and giving a smile that seemed like a leer. "Certainly I call that war. And war is so often folly—so often sheer folly, my dear Harold."

Harold had to gather his thoughts resolutely together. He must not prematurely give away his intentions. The man stooping to the marble slab was obviously not in immediate fear of an attempt being made on his life, or he would not divide his attentions between his chemical experiments and his intending assassin. But

Harold had to keep himself keenly on the alert so as to be ready to shoot and make no error.

"And often sheer necessity," he retorted, while the woman outside called, "Teeny, Teeny, Teeny, Teeny!"

"Be that as it may," said Michel Benni, "it is first advisable to know the strength of one's enemy. Is that not so?"

"Or the strength of one's own hand. If that—"

Michel Benni ignored the remark.

"I am performing an interesting experiment," he said. "Have you any knowledge of medicine?"

"No."

"Nor of the occult arts?"

"No."

"I see you do not smile when I mention the occult arts. That is something. Many people do not take occult matters seriously. They do not believe in the devil, for instance, and they smile at the thought of alchemists and those who sought the *elixir vitae.* Well, let them laugh while they may. Your sister, my dear Harold, takes these things seriously. She believes that nothing is impossible—nothing."

"Yes," Harold replied. "And that's why I'm here now. I don't like the idea of my sister believing that nothing is impossible. It isn't the kind of thing that sane people do believe."

"I see that we differ in our notions of sanity," Michel Benni remarked. "You no doubt believe that time never stands still, for instance? And I should be surprised if you were to allow that a man could be in two places, far apart, at the same moment."

Harold laughed, mirthlessly and with a touch of scorn.

"Ah, well!" Michel Benni murmured, turning again to the chemical work he had in hand. "You will believe in these things some day. To-morrow, perhaps. Who knows? You will also believe that one can love and fear the same object at the same time. Does that mean anything to you, my dear Harold?"

"No, it doesn't."

"That is strange," said Michel Benni. "It means such a great deal to your sister. For instance," he went on, "she lives in fear of me. She lives in a state of horror because she knows I have dealings with the devil and because she has been made to feel the powers of darkness. She knows that she will in time go mad—as you are pleased to call it—unless she can resist my fascination. Yet she does not resist. She does not try to resist. Is not that the fusing of two opposite emotions, my dear Harold? The mixing of oil with water, which you would say to be impossible?"

"No," Harold cried, taking a quick step forward. "That's plain hypnotism. That's what it is—hypnotism. I thought it might be that. You've hypnotized her, and she can't help herself. I know enough about the black arts to see that now. You've managed to get her will under your control, and you can make her do what you want her to do and think what you want her to think."

Michel Benni took little notice of the young man's words and manner, startling though they might be. He merely glanced up with the calm smile of self-assurance that was typical of him.

"You may be partly right," he said. "Not that it matters. Your slight knowledge can be of no use to your sister. Of course, I know why you came here to-night . . ."

Harold tried resolutely to control himself, but control was difficult in the face of that casually uttered remark. It was as though he had been struck a painful blow on the mouth.

"You came to kill me," Michel Benni went on. "I think I guess correctly. But you might ask why I do not take steps to protect myself. And to that I answer that it is not necessary. When we spoke about being at war, I mentioned that it was advisable first to know the strength of one's enemy. I made that remark because I was convinced that you had no conception of my power. You think it is merely a question of drawing a knife and plunging it into my back, or shooting me with a pistol. But no, my dear Harold, these things are not so simply done . . . You see, I give you a good opportunity, but still you hesitate."

Harold knew what the man meant, but he also knew that the man was mistaken. Michel Benni was apparently relying upon that strange, frightening power, inherent in his very manner, which had a deterring effect on any who desired to oppose him. Harold had felt that power; he felt it now. It was that and similar powers, seeming to emanate from the man, that had first made Harold suspect his abnormality. But if the fellow thought that, by the mere exertion of his will or by the mere strength of his personality, he was going to stop Harold from doing what he came here to do, then he was greatly mistaken. Harold had Cynthia to consider. He was here to save her from being sent mad by this man's devilish influence, and the desire to save her was stronger than anything else that could affect him.

He knew what hypnotism was, and he knew that you could be caught and held by a hypnotic stare only if you relaxed your vigilance sufficiently. As long as he avoided the man's eyes he would be safe; but once he allowed his thoughts to stray beyond the strict control of his own will—went wool-gathering or daydreaming—he might find it difficult at first, and presently impossible, to bring his thoughts back; they would have gone beyond his control and would be held in the power of the hypnotist who could direct them, and so direct the physical body related to them, to his own purpose.

In the case of Cynthia, of course, Michel Benni's task had probably been a very easy one. Cynthia had suspected nothing, for she had not had any warning whatsoever of the man's powers, and so he had been able to hypnotize her without having to contend with any opposition on her part—probably when he was carrying on an innocent conversation with her, Harold reflected.

And from that moment she was at his mercy.

The horror of that now struck him forcibly; Michel Benni had virtually admitted that hypnotism was the basis of his power over Cynthia; but, even if he had not admitted it, his comments were sufficiently explicit. Like most badly-balanced persons he was boastful regarding such powers as he possessed, and in boasting of the fact that Cynthia was attracted towards him, even while she regarded him with fear and horror, he had made plain enough the reason for his hold over her.

Harold knew just enough about this dark business to be acutely aware of Cynthia's plight. She had known Michel Benni now for over two months, and, as repetitions of the hypnotic process ever weakened and weakened her will-power and ever strengthened Michel Benni's control over her, there could be no doubt that she was now completely under his domination. He had but to will her to do a certain thing and she would do it. She might not wish to do it; she might not know why she was doing it; but towards doing it she would feel a mysterious urge that was irresistible.

And this man had boasted about his having brought Cynthia to such a plight! For that alone he deserved death. And if his death was not justified from vindictiveness, it was nevertheless justified on account of his boasting, because that very boasting showed in what an irresponsible way he used his dark weapons; and it followed almost certainly that he would utterly ignore the terrible distress of his victim in his warped desire to feel his own powers.

An appeal to his better nature to release Cynthia from her dreadful bondage would be doomed to failure for the simple reason that he had no better nature to which an appeal might be made.

That was already proved by his having brought Cynthia to her present condition of fear, and, in any case, Harold was not going to take such risks as might be involved by delays. He was going to strike now in the only certain way he knew.

If only that woman with her confounded "Teeny, Teeny!" would go indoors!

"Yes, as I mentioned before, I am hoping to carry through a most interesting experiment to-night," said the scientist, seeming to give little enough heed to the likelihood of his being shot dead at any moment. "Perhaps you will be good enough to assist me—yes?"

"I certainly shan't," said Harold.

"Oh, but I beg of you!" Michel Benni pleaded, while a disturbing glint of amusement showed in the glance that he turned towards Harold. "You might find it rather pleasant," he went on. "You will certainly find it interesting. And you will not have to wait very long to learn the result of the experiment. It is not one of those tedious matters that require an infinity of patience. We shall have to wait no longer than to-morrow in order to learn the result—to-morrow, or the next day at the latest."

"I'm not interested in your experiments," said Harold. "Or if I am interested it is only in the matter of putting an end to them."

He was still standing some feet away from the other man. His left hand held his hat; his right was in the pocket of his overcoat, where it gripped the now warm butt of the revolver, fingering the trigger-guard and taking added confidence from the general solidity of the weapon.

"You are a very rash young man," said Michel Benni.

Harold privately agreed that he was. He felt that he ought not to have so finally intimated his intentions.

"I can afford to be rash," he said, making the most of the situation. "You see, I have now got your measure. I know your strength, and I know that though you can exert your influence over my sister, you can't exert your influence over me. I know that you are only a hypnotist, in spite of all your talk about black magic, and I know how to keep out of your range. You want me to help you with some experiment or other. You think that if I agree, you will have a chance of tricking me into letting you hypnotize me or something of the sort."

He paused, and remained for a few moments in an attitude of listening.

A minor commotion was going on outside. Teeny had at last answered the call and was being scolded and fondled, smacked and loved by his mistress. Then the sounds became less and less distinct. A door banged. A radio started to shout into the night. A car with a cylinder that missed swept along Gurlitt Row.

Harold, in a flash, took his revolver from his overcoat pocket and fired point-blank at Michel Benni's chest.

For a fraction of a second the man's eyes showed fear. But there was no time for him to do anything. The glance of fear was almost immediately extinguished as he fell back against the marble slab. It was replaced by a dead stare. Harold fired again as the body slipped to the floor.

The first shot had smashed the breastbone, by the look of it, for the shirt was already stained with blood; but even at that point-blank range Harold had not been able to resist the impulse to shoot again. It had not occurred to him to try to make the death look like suicide, which he might conceivably have done by firing only one shot, then letting the revolver fall to the floor near the body. His sole thought had been to make doubly sure that the man was dead and that Cynthia was freed from the curse that hung over her.

He did not think, for instance, that one revolver shot might pass almost without comment but that two could hardly be expected to do so.

He thrust the revolver back into his pocket, glanced once—rather fearfully—at the body that lay in an awkward position on the floor, then turned towards the exit from the laboratory.

In spite of all his reasoning, he was afraid because of what he had done. But he was not in a panic. He was fully alert to his own danger, and there was no risk of his landing himself on the scaffold from lack of prudence.

He remembered that he had touched nothing except the bell-push at the front door. And before touching anything now he put on his gloves. The key of the laboratory was on the inside of the lock. He removed it, then opened the door. Before switching off the light he glanced round the place. The windows, of which there were six or eight, had their glass covered with a thin coating of whitewash or distemper, either to ensure privacy or to diffuse the light during the daytime. The body lay partly under the long marble slab and close to a pile of variously-shaped packing-cases that had probably contained chemicals and scientific instruments. It was safe to assume that the body would not be discovered for a day or two, unless a window were to be accidentally broken and someone should peep in.

That would not matter very much, of course, Harold reflected; but on general principles it would be as well to delay the discovery as long as possible so as to make it more difficult for the authorities to determine the exact time of death. He therefore moved some of the empty packing-cases in order to conceal the body completely, turned off the gas under the iron vessel, switched out the light, and departed from the laboratory, locking the door after him and putting the key into his pocket.

He would fling the key into the river before the night was out. In the meantime, he had but to pass through the sitting-room and let himself out by the front door. He must not forget to moisten his glove and lightly rub the bell-push in order to remove any possible fingerprint. And, of course, he would throw his revolver into the river as well.

After that no evidence could possibly connect him with the death of Michel Benni.

CHAPTER VI

AGENT OF NEMESIS

HE GOT OUT of the house without being observed by any of the inmates, and presently descended to the pavement, which was now deserted but for one man who happened to be hurrying past.

It occurred to Harold to hang back a little until this man should actually have passed the house, but at the same instant he told himself that to do so would be to assume a fugitive air, so that his very desire for concealment would draw attention to himself. He therefore stepped out to the pavement and set off briskly, concealing himself under the cloak of innocent normality.

But this was a case in which wisdom of action did not meet with the success it deserved. The pedestrian hesitated in his stride and, after an instant's pause, exclaimed:

"Hallo, Crossland! What are you doing here?" Harold had the feeling that Nemesis had already overtaken him. The unexpectedness of the other man's greeting had about it the force of doom, and that no less because the man was only the most casual of acquaintances. He was a fellow belonging to Harold's club—by name Wyldebore—and, as far as Harold knew, never had occasion to visit Bloomsbury, and might never be expected to be seen in Gurlitt Row.

Yet, he was here at this fatal moment! In a day or two perhaps, Harold reflected, Gurlitt Row would be in the front of the news. And Wyldebore would remember this moment and would be ready to talk about it.

"Hallo, old chap!" Harold replied, putting cordiality into his tone, albeit he felt that his face was bloodless. "What are *you* doing here?"

They had stopped exactly outside the house that Harold had just left. He saw Wyldebore glance interestedly at the place, and could not doubt that his glance took in the number that was painted in large white figures on the stonework adjoining the doorway.

And he saw Wyldebore's glance move from the doorway to himself—to his old overcoat and battered hat.

These were a mistake. He ought not to have tried to conceal himself by trying to appear to be other than he was. The old overcoat and the battered hat were suspicious, and would make Wyldebore wonder.

Wyldebore explained that he was cutting through this way to call on some Bohemian friends of his who lived just round the corner. Harold advanced the information, as lightly as he could, that he had been paying a visit of charity. It was the first thing he could think of that would explain his being there, and it seemed to satisfy Wyldebore, who stood talking for a few moments longer, then took his leave and went on his way.

But Harold knew that the explanation would not satisfy Wyldebore when the murdered body of Michel Benni should be found. And as he walked away he found himself to be trembling. He felt that he had been suddenly caught in a maze. He experienced panic. It was the old story. He had guarded against all reasonable miscarriages, but the million-to-one chance had intervened and he was thrown into a totally new set of circumstances for which he had made no provision.

Had he been seen by one of the inmates of the house it would not have mattered. No one there had ever set eyes upon him before, so he would only be described as an unknown man who had visited the place at a certain time.

Yes, it was panic that was making him tremble—panic at the thought that he had gone so far only to find his way blocked, and himself hemmed in by a set of damning circumstances. The body of Michel Benni would be found, and he would be associated with it. That was inevitable—inevitable. He broke into a run, hastening back towards the lights of Tottenham Court Road. He wanted to run and run. Fortunately there was no one about to see him, for his face was a deathly white and his eyes were staring.

After a few moments he realized that he must pull himself together. He must face the situation reasonably. The unexpected appearance of Wyldebore was one of those supremely ironic gestures of fate designed to bring about utter confusion and to make a man forget caution and act on wild impulse.

But Harold held his instincts in check. Flight, he knew, would be of no use. He must face the situation and try to make some order out of chaos.

Presently he hailed a taxi, and directed the driver to Forbes' address in Regent Street.

It took even Forbes some time to grasp the full significance of the situation. Forbes went white on first hearing the news, and his cold blue eyes stared at Harold Crossland as though it were Crossland and not fate that had brought the threat—almost the certainty—of disaster upon them.

When he found his voice, it was a voice barely recognizable as his.

"Don't get into a panic," he said. "Keep cool. Don't get into a panic. That's the principal thing."

He got Harringay and Mathers on the telephone, and presently they arrived, one following closely upon the heels of the other. Harringay, usually calm and philosophical and given to belittling danger, had a serious frown on his face. Mathers' lips were trembling and he could not remain still, but kept walking about the room until Forbes told him angrily to sit down.

"We're safe until the body is found," Forbes pointed out. "That's an advantage that we might have been denied."

"Until the body is found . . ." Mathers murmured in a hoarse voice.

"Oh, you're no good, Mathers!" Harringay exclaimed, with a glance at Forbes, who was the natural leader of the group.

"I'm sorry," said Mathers. "You see, I've never been mixed up with a murder before. It's—it's hell."

"Hell's the word," Forbes agreed. "And it's better that you should realize that. It means that you've got to keep your head. We're all in it. Crossland did it, but we're all in it. And if one lets his nerve get the better of him, we're all dished."

Mathers did not answer, but he glanced surreptitiously at the other three, one after another.

"We've got to remove the body before it's found," Harringay said. "That strikes me as being the obvious thing to do."

"I'm not going back there," Harold Crossland cried. "I couldn't go back there."

"And what good would it do anyway?" Mathers asked. "Put the body into the Thames, eh? And what good will that do? It'll be found sooner or later."

"Exactly," said Forbes. "It'll be found sooner or later. And when it is found, the whole truth will come out. The date of his last appearance alive. The place—Gurlitt Row. The sound of two revolver shots. The fact of Crossland leaving the house just shortly after the revolver shots were heard. We needn't hope that those things won't come to light. They will. You can trust the police for that. So what does that suggest to you?"

Mathers, his fingers twitching, looked up excitedly.

"It suggests that we had better clear out—quick," he said eagerly. "We've got a day—perhaps two days—you said. We can get a long way off in two days." Harringay coughed.

"If you think we can get beyond the reach of Scotland Yard in two days," he said, "you don't know much about Scotland Yard."

Mathers hid his face in his hands.

"We've got to get the body away from there—that's definite," said Forbes. "What's to happen after that I don't know, but we've got to get the body away from there. The point to be recognized, however," he went on, "is that the body must not be found anywhere. We can't simply take it away and dump it in a ditch somewhere. That would be all right if we only wanted to get it off our hands. But we must do more than that. The moment the police learn that the man has been murdered we're done for."

"I see that," said Harringay. "So we must hide the body."

"That's it," Forbes agreed. "We must hide the body."

"Where?" Mathers asked.

"Where it can never be found," Forbes replied. "I suggest that we take it right out to sea and drop it overboard, in really deep water, with plenty of weights tied to its feet. Enough weights to keep it anchored to the bottom. The fishes will do the rest."

Harold Crossland took an eager step forward.

"That's it!" he exclaimed. "The bottom of the sea!"

"The safest place I know," said Forbes.

"The only safe place," Harold asserted, speaking, it seemed, with unnecessary conviction.

"Buried in a grave six feet deep would be just as safe," said Harringay. "But the sea is the best place," he added. "More convenient, at any rate."

"No, it must be the sea—the bottom of the sea," Harold maintained. "And lots of weights. Lots of weights. I'm afraid of that man."

"But he's dead!" Forbes exclaimed. Mathers rose suddenly, clasping his head in his hands.

"That's the trouble—he's dead!" he whined, with a nervous tremor in his voice.

"Sit down!" Forbes commanded. "You know what we'll do with anyone who loses his head. At least, you can guess."

He fixed Mathers with a steady gaze. Mathers sat down again, making an effort to compose himself.

"Dead or not dead, I'm afraid of him, I tell you," Harold persisted. "I don't know why. I just am. Do you believe in black magic?"

"Another one got 'em!" said Harringay. "Though I suppose there's some excuse for you, Crossland. You killed him. Have a drink."

"It isn't only that I killed him," Harold retorted, turning towards the sideboard but being forestalled by Forbes, who removed the stopper from the whisky decanter. "It isn't only that I killed him. That's bad enough, but it isn't that. It's something about the man. I don't know what it is. I said he was insane. And he was. But it wasn't the ordinary insanity. Do you think that people can be in league with the devil? When he's at the bottom of the sea I'll feel safe. Why should Wyldebore pass the house just as I was coming out? Wyldebore said it was the first time he had ever been in that street. Why should he go there just at that time? Do you think some mysterious intelligence about which we know nothing could have influenced him? Michel Benni said—"

"Here! Drink this!" Forbes interrupted him. "Drink as much as you like—both of you. And when you can't stand any longer, you'll find that those settees make very comfortable beds. When you wake up—Oh, give me the key of that laboratory, will you, Crossland!—When you wake up you'll feel much better—both of you—in every way. Harringay and I will see about—about the other."

Forbes exchanged a look with Harringay, who nodded.

"He's got some packing cases there, did you say?" he asked.

"All sorts and sizes," Harold answered. "Can you take the body out to sea to-night?"

"You leave it to us," Forbes advised him.

"But can you?" Harold persisted. "To-night? Can you do it to-night?"

"You needn't be scared by a dead body," Harringay put in.

"I'm not scared by a dead body," Harold protested. "But there was something strange about that man—"

"Finish up your drink and have another—and another," Forbes advised. "And don't leave this flat, either of you. And don't answer the door, should anybody ring. You'll get us all hanged—the state you're in. Keep calm. I'll see about hiring a boat to-morrow. By tomorrow night we'll all be as safe as houses . . ."

CHAPTER VII

THE BATHROOM CUPBOARD

THE SMOULDERING-EYED Forbes and the big, shapeless Harringay undertook the removal of the body without any particular distaste. To neither was there anything especially repulsive about a dead body as such. In the present case, the dead body represented danger while it remained where it was, and that was their greatest concern.

Ten minutes later the two men were in Forbes' car, which he had brought from a garage close to the flat. They spoke but little as Forbes drove quickly towards Bloomsbury and Gurlitt Row. Such remarks as passed between them were mainly in reference to the emotional reactions of the two younger members of the quartet.

Forbes, in three words, sought to bring upon their heads the curse of divine condemnation; then he went on to say that that was the worst of landing on the wrong side of the law in the company of a couple whose nerves gave out at the very mention of a dead body.

"Mathers is no good, I'll grant that," said Harringay. "Pity he had to be in it. But there's some excuse for Crossland."

"Yes, it's a pity Mathers had to be in it, all right," said Forbes. "And we needn't have had him. We wouldn't have had if I'd thought the girl would throw him over. But it was all nice and comfortable—the girl's brother, the girl's boy friend, and us."

"And the girl's money."

"Oh, and the girl's money, of course!" Forbes murmured, accompanying the murmur with a smile that seemed to reflect his secret thoughts. "In six months—if the girl doesn't begin interfering before then—we'll have doubled the capital she entrusted to us."

"Or it will have vanished down a drain."

"True! There is that risk. But we stand to make about thirty thousand on the gamble."

"And she stands to lose about the same amount if our gamble isn't successful. But I'm almost sure it will be successful. And so long as these two don't get the jim-jams too badly—"

"It's only Mathers you've got to be afraid of. Crossland's all right. He had enough nerve to go and do the murder, anyway. I couldn't have trusted Mathers to do it. Granted he's on edge now—Crossland, I mean—but it's the first time he's killed a man. He didn't flinch last night, when the cards went against him. He'll be better by the morning."

"I'm not so sure about that," Forbes replied. "I didn't like the way he spoke about being afraid of the dead man. When they begin to talk like that, they've got to be handled very carefully—or very drastically. They're dangerous. They're in the mood for believing all they've ever heard about dead people coming back to haunt their late enemies—especially murdered people coming back to haunt their murderers."

"Oh, he'll get over it," Harringay murmured. "He had an idea that the man was abnormal; that probably makes it worse. But he'll get over it."

"We all know that the man was abnormal," Forbes replied, "but he wasn't so abnormal as to give me the impression that he would be more dangerous dead than alive. That's the kind of notion that has got hold of Crossland, isn't it?"

"But he doesn't mean it like that," Harringay pointed out. "He means that we're more unsafe with Benni dead than we were with Benni alive. And that, of course, is perfectly true. Our necks weren't in danger while Benni was alive. That's what Crossland means."

"Here's the place," said Forbes, turning a corner unexpectedly and dropping the speed of the car. "I don't think he means that. He gave me the impression—But it doesn't matter. It's a shock for him, as you say, and he'll probably get over it by the morning. But we'll have to silence Mathers if *he* doesn't pull himself together."

He mounted the few steps to the door of the house and, without hesitation, pressed a bell-push. His manner was cool and self-possessed and disarming. The ease with which he had tripped up the steps, throwing back his overcoat and feeling in his trousers pockets for the key that Crossland had given him, was in every detail the manner of a man who was engaged in perfectly innocent business.

The ring was answered by an elderly woman, who had switched on a light during her passage through the narrow hall.

"Thanks so much!" said Forbes, and stepped over the threshold. "Turning foggy again. This way, old chap. The laboratory's out at the back. The Professor told you we were coming, of course?"

He addressed this last remark to the old woman, who looked nervously puzzled and muttered something that the two men did not catch.

"He sent us along for some chemicals and instruments," Forbes went on. "He gave us the key of the laboratory, but forgot the key of the front door. Did he say the things were packed, old chap?"

"No, we've to pack them," Harringay grumbled. "Said we would find plenty of wooden cases."

"Oh, Lor'!" Forbes murmured, shrugging his shoulders. "Well, we're sorry to have troubled you, ma'am," he went on in a different voice. "Thanks very much."

With that he turned, barely looking where he was going, and opened the door of Michel Benni's sitting-room. His air of having done the same thing a hundred times before would have imposed upon an infinitely more suspicious person than the old caretaker or landlady of the place.

Presently they were through in the laboratory. Forbes entered first. He was a comparatively short man, and he could walk as noiselessly as a cat, and with the same dangerous significance to anyone who knew his character. To those who did not know his character his delicately-shod feet, his neat style of deportment, and his carefully-smoothed black hair indicated merely a man who took exceeding interest in his personal appearance.

Harringay closed the door of the laboratory and remained near it while Forbes stepped over to the rampart of packing-cases that hid the body. To Harringay, Forbes' face was in profile as he inclined his figure a little forward to look over the rampart.

Only the faintest grimace of distaste showed on that face.

He glanced at Harringay.

"We'll have to clean up the blood," he said.

Harringay advanced and looked. The body lay awkwardly as it had happened to fall. Of course, Crossland wouldn't have touched it. It was surprising that Crossland had had the nerve to pile these cases round it. It must have been the meeting with that fellow outside that had sent Crossland dithery.

"The bleeding has stopped now, anyway," he said. "And rigor mortis hasn't set in yet, of course."

"He's a big man," Forbes observed. "We'll have to see that the case is strong enough."

He started to examine the boxes and cases.

"It needn't be long and narrow, like a coffin," said Harringay. "As rigor mortis hasn't set in yet—Here's one with rope handles. A solid one. But the lid's loose."

"As long as it has a lid of some sort—We mustn't spend too much time here."

The box selected was slightly longer than it was wide, and was about two feet deep. To move the inert body was not an easy matter, and was made more difficult because of the care required to prevent blood from being transferred to the outside of the box or to the men's clothes. But the ponderous, sagging mass was at length placed safely in position. They covered it with a white overall that had been lying near at hand, and that, in turn, they covered and completely hid with a quantity of shavings. Then they placed the lid on top.

Harringay cleaned the floor. He did it very thoroughly, while Forbes urged him to hurry. Forbes pointed out that there would be no microscopic examination by the police, because there would never be any mention of murder. They would tell the landlady, in a day or two, that her distinguished tenant had gone abroad; then they would pay any rent that might by agreement be due, and remove the rest of the contents of the laboratory, acting ostensibly as Michel Benni's assistants.

But Harringay took very great pains with the washing of the small patch of floor on to which blood had trickled.

"Perhaps it's as well that we have to remove the body," he said, as he wrung the cloth out thoroughly into an elaborate sink that had been fitted at the front of the marble slab. "It means that there needn't be any enquiry, as you say, and that there needn't be the faintest risk to ourselves. But we want to take every precaution in case there should be an enquiry."

"I say, *you* aren't going nervy, are you?" Forbes asked, with a keen glance at his companion.

"Nervy?"

"Yes, nervy . . . That's the worst of a pair like Mathers and Crossland. One gets into a panic and sets the other off. And now you! . . . I tell you the body will have half a mile of sea water on top of it by this time to-morrow night."

"Oh, *I'm* not getting scared."

"That's all right then. I thought that perhaps Crossland's hint about being afraid of the body—"

"Crossland meant afraid of the *evidence* that the body might provide."

"So you said. But I think he meant more than that. In short, I think he's ready to believe anything . . . We'd better be off. It's going to be a weight—this case of chemical appliances."

Less than half an hour later they were carrying the case up the stairway that led to Forbes' flat. They entered the flat silently, though with a certain awkwardness, and moved through to the bathroom, Forbes walking backwards with short, shuffling steps, Harringay breathing quickly, and the solid weight of the case bearing down between them.

It was with relief that they laid the case on the bathroom floor, pushed it into a cupboard, then straightened their backs. Harringay mopped his forehead with a handkerchief. Forbes divested himself of his overcoat and jacket, and washed his hands. Harringay did the same. The delicate scent of the soap was pleasant, and the feel of the water was refreshing. Presently they went through to the sitting-room.

Crossland had not been drinking, but Mathers had. Crossland was pacing back and forth on the carpet. Mathers was sitting nodding dazedly in an easy chair. Crossland turned quickly and stared as the door opened.

"You fellows had better get to sleep," said Forbes. "We've brought the body away. Everything's safe now."

"Where is it?" Crossland asked, still staring.

"In a box in the bathroom. Have some whisky and get to bed. You too, Mathers."

"I can't go home," said Crossland. "Cynthia would know there was something wrong."

"I'll take good care that you don't attempt to go home—either of you," said Forbes. "You'll both stay here till you've got your nerve back. A sleep will do you good."

Crossland's expression showed profound fear.

"I couldn't sleep," he said. "I'm—I'm afraid to go to sleep. I might dream. Why didn't you tell me?"

"Tell you what?"

"Tell me that murder was like this."

"Like what?"

"Like this. Hasn't it got any significance for you—any superstitious significance? Don't you believe in *anything,* Forbes? Have you ever done a murder?"

"I'll do one in a minute if you don't take a tight grip on yourself, Crossland. Here, fill up, chaps! Mathers, fill up and come and have a game of cards. There are some sandwiches in the larder, Harringay . . . You don't want to be scared now—any of you. The body's safe. Let's have something to eat and drink, and deal the cards for poker."

CHAPTER VIII

EDDIE DINES FROM HOME

AT a few minutes before seven o'clock that evening, Eddie Landor strode into the drawing-room of the parental home in Holland Park, W. His mother and sister sat there, each with a book. His father had not yet finished dressing, but would be down presently.

"His lordship deigns to dine with us," said Susie without looking up from her book. "Why don't you ask him to sit down, mother!"

Eddie picked up a cushion, stood surveying his sister unsmilingly for a space of five seconds, then put the cushion back again.

"I saw you," said Susie, still with her gaze fixed on her book. "And if you'd thrown it it would have cost you five shillings."

"Isn't it about time somebody invented a permanent complexion?" he asked.

"But you would probably have missed," she commented. "So it wouldn't have cost you anything . . . Why don't you ask him to sit down, mother?"

"He can sit down without invitation, I'm sure."

Susie put her book aside.

"But don't you realize that he hasn't dined with us for a week?" she asked. "Here, let me offer you a chair."

She made as though to rise, but her brother, still unsmiling, gripped her firmly by the shoulder with one muscular hand and forced her back again.

"Oh, Eddie!" she screamed. "That hurts. Your fingers—"

"Now, now, children!" said their mother.

"There, you see!" Susie murmured. "You're getting me into a scrape now. Behave yourself. Come and sit beside me and tell me what you've been doing with yourself lately. There's a girl in the case, of course?"

"Susie—" her mother murmured in mild admonition.

"But, mother, of course there's a girl in the case," Susie protested. "And we only hope she's nice. Is she nice, Eddie?"

"Susie—" her mother admonished once more. "Your father will

be down in a minute."

"Well, what's that got to do with it, mother?"

"You ought to behave more respectably."

"Respectably? Oh, isn't that beautifully Victorian, Eddie? Just as though father never dined away from home for a whole week on end when he was your age! Who was the girl in the case then? Oh, the naughty 'nineties!"

"Shall I pinch her, mother?"

"Behave yourselves—both of you. And, anyway, it wasn't the 'nineties."

"All right, mother; she can't count," Eddie explained. "You see, my girl," he went on, turning to his sister, "in the 'nineties mother was still at school—"

"Well, what about that?"

"I wish you two would discuss your own affairs."

"That's what we were doing, mother," Susie pointed out. "But you suggested they weren't respectable. Surely you don't mean that yours aren't respectable, either!"

"I can see I'll have to do something," said Eddie, adopting a threatening attitude.

"Mother! Stop him! He's going to ruffle my hair and I've just—Eddie, don't! That hurts. Your hands are made of iron. There's the telephone. Go and answer it. Good!"

Eddie strolled out into the hall and picked up the receiver.

"Yes," he said, affirming a question regarding his identity. "Oh, you're Cynthia! Splendid! And you've decided to marry me, eh?"

This unexpected call caused him to wonder. He spoke facetiously from habit, but in his mind he was uneasy.

"I wonder if I can see you, Eddie?" Cynthia asked, ignoring his light remark. "Can we have dinner somewhere? Have you had dinner?"

"Come along here," he suggested eagerly. "You haven't met the family yet. They'll be pleased."

"Thanks, Eddie," she replied. "But I can't—to-night. I want to see you alone. I should love to meet your family. But I couldn't stand up to anything like that to-night. Something—something dreadful has happened."

"Something dreadful? What? What has happened?"

"I can't speak about it on the telephone. Can't I see you? At a restaurant? Have you seen Harold to-night?"

"No. But I don't understand—"

"I wonder where he is. Oh, Eddie, I'm so afraid. Do let me see you. I must tell somebody."

"Right!" he answered. "Where are you? Where shall I meet you?"

He could not guess what had happened. He could not be sure, in fact, that anything had happened. Remembering Cynthia Crossland as she had been on the previous night, when she had imagined a full hour to pass within the actual space of two minutes, he had to mistrust any startling statement she might make.

The something dreadful, however, was real enough to her, as he could tell by the tone of fear in which she spoke, and that was bad enough. In fact, it was possibly worse than an actually dreadful occurrence. Last night he had been made to realize very intensely some of the awful possibilities of the human mind. Like most healthy people, he had always been apt to sneer at what were termed imaginary ailments, arguing subconsciously that the dam' fool of a patient could cure himself simply by ceasing to imagine that he was ill.

But imaginary ailments were much more serious than that. They were, indeed, much more serious than real ailments. Real ailments manifested themselves physically and their presence and progress could be observed. But imaginary ailments manifested themselves only to the sufferers Everyone else knew them to be imaginary; only the sufferers knew them to be real. For, of course, to them they were real. Nothing that is known can be known except in the mind. Things seen, things touched, things heard—these exist as phenomena only when the mind becomes aware of them. And, inversely, what the mind is aware of does virtually exist, although it might have no physical actuality.

So what Cynthia might imagine to be fact would be, to her, fact.

She eagerly mentioned a certain restaurant, and Eddie as eagerly agreed to meet her there. He returned to the drawing-room.

"His lordship isn't dining with us after all, mother," Susie announced. "And her name is Cynthia."

"You were listening."

"Aren't you good at guessing, Eddie! But you shouldn't leave the door open if you would be private. So her name is Cynthia, eh?"

"That happens to be the name of the person who telephoned."

"Oh, you mustn't call her a person, Eddie! She wouldn't like that. I know I shouldn't. But why won't she dine with us? I heard you asking her."

"She can't to-night," Eddie said, inconclusively. "But she will soon, I hope."

He wanted to tell his mother and Susie—but especially Susie—all about Cynthia and about the man, Michel Benni; but he could not see how he could do so without giving the impression that Cynthia was not one who could be held responsible for her thoughts and actions. And the healthy sanity of the house in Holland Park, W., would receive a shock if it were to be thought that the son and heir had for his special friend a girl who saw visions and dreamed dreams.

He got out of the house without having to come down to particulars regarding his friendship with Cynthia, got his car out of the garage and set off for the West End.

He was not really troubling himself with trying to guess what had happened according to Cynthia's belief. He was concerned only with making another attempt to discover what was really wrong with Cynthia. Since the previous night, there had been growing upon him the conviction that if she were free of influence or coercion, he himself would not have to ask her very much oftener whether she would marry him. And that conviction had now been encouraged by the fact of her telephoning to him—to him particularly—in order to disburden her mind. So, in undertaking to destroy whatever it might be that was hanging over her head, he had every hope of his own reward.

He wondered whether matters would have taken the same course had he proposed to Cynthia earlier. They assuredly would not, he reflected, as he raced along Bayswater Road in the direction of the Marble Arch. The merest pebble dropped into the stream of life alters the course of numerous particles of that stream, and his own advent into the life of Cynthia would certainly have altered her life so far as its hour by hour progress was concerned, and it might be reasoned with some assurance that she would not have met Michel Benni, for the meeting, Eddie understood, had been purely accidental.

However, regrets were of no use now. He could only set himself resolutely to get to the bottom of the matter and try to put it right. Michel Benni was the man to be dealt with, and Eddie, as he parked his car preparatory to entering the restaurant, hoped that he might be able to induce Cynthia to arrange a meeting with this Michel Benni.

CHAPTER IX

ANOTHER PROPOSAL

"EDDIE," SHE SAID, in a voice that was hushed and that vibrated with intensity, "Michel Benni's dead. Harold killed him."

Eddie regarded her searchingly. The announcement that some person—any person whom you know, but particularly one who has been playing a vital part among your circle of acquaintances—is dead is a sufficiently startling announcement. That he has been killed by the brother of the girl you hope to marry is infinitely more startling. But Eddie's reactions fell far short of what might have been expected.

He tried to show amazement. He even tried to appear to be shocked. But it was almost wholly pretence. He did not believe that Harold had killed Michel Benni. He did not even believe that Michel Benni was dead.

Yet, Cynthia might be speaking from reliable knowledge.

"When was this?" he asked.

"About ten minutes before I telephoned to you," Cynthia said.

"You telephoned from your home, didn't you?"

"Yes."

"Did it happen there?"

"No. It happened in the laboratory—Michel Benni's laboratory."

"That's in Bloomsbury somewhere, isn't it?"

"Yes."

"Then how did you learn about it so quickly?"

She did not reply immediately. They were seated by this time at a small table laid for two. She had remained silent regarding the announcement she had to make until the order for the dinner had been given and the first course brought to the table. When she arrived in the foyer of the restaurant, Eddie had thought that her expression was more normal than it had been on the previous night; she was uneasy about something, he had guessed, but even her uneasiness was preferable to her late strangeness. Nevertheless, he could not take her seriously when she said that Harold had killed Michel Benni.

"I don't know," she said at length. "I just knew that it was going to happen. Then I knew that it had happened."

Eddie frowned. He had no wish to learn that Harold Crossland was a murderer, but he was at the same time disappointed to know that Cynthia was still seeing visions.

"Tell me about it," he said. "We must see what we can do."

"About saving Harold, you mean?"

"Yes, about saving Harold. That, of course, is the first thing."

"That is the whole thing," she stated. "That's what is troubling me—the risk that Harold has taken. You are surprised, Eddie. Or shocked. You think I ought to be horrified about it."

"Well—"

"But I'm not, Eddie. I'm not shocked at the idea of murder. I'm only afraid for Harold. I know why he did it. I think it was very brave of him. He did it because he didn't like Michel Benni. Rather, because he would have done anything to prevent me from marrying Michel Benni. We had some dreadful quarrels about that—Harold and I. But he was right and I was wrong. I know it now. I didn't think so then. He made some terrible allegations against Michel Benni. He said he was insane and that he would send me insane. He said he was sending me insane already. I couldn't see what grounds Harold had for thinking things like that. I thought he was only afraid because Michel Benni was such a powerful man. Powerful in intellectual force, I mean. I thought Harold didn't understand him, and that he suspected him of having some fearful purpose in cultivating my acquaintance. He said he was sending me mad just for the fun of the thing. But even now—when I feel that I can think clearly about the whole matter—I'm sure Michel Benni would not send me mad just for the fun of the thing. Of course, he wasn't sending me mad at all. It was only that I was falling into his way of thinking. But that doesn't matter now. Only, I'm not sorry that he's dead. I think I feel relieved. I don't know. His noticing me was a great honour. I don't suppose you can understand. He was, I think, the most powerful man in the world and he wanted me to share his position. He had planned to found a race that would become masters of the world, and I would be their queen, he said. And I believed him. I still believe that he could do what he said he could do. It would be a race of monsters, I gathered. It was frightening, but I felt that it would be tremendously thrilling. And besides that, time would not matter, for he and I and all the rest would just live on and on. That is why we would be able to become masters of the whole world. But I'm not sorry that he is dead. It is better to be normal and live an ordinary life. Do you understand what I have been talking about?"

Eddie pretended that he did understand. There could be no point, he thought, in asking her to clarify her statements, even assuming that she could do so. Nor could there be any point in arguing that people—even such supposedly wonderful people as Michel Benni—could live on and on. And if her story about Harold's having murdered Michel Benni had any truth in it, the lie was immediately given to any claim he may have put forward in the matter of possessing the gift of eternal life.

"But that is all past now," she went on. "And I'm glad. Yes, I'm more glad than I can tell you. Do you know what morbid fascination is? You know what the words mean, of course; but have you ever experienced what they mean? Morbid fascination such as Michel Benni could incite would lead to madness in time. Harold was right. The man was mad—mad with the singleness of purpose that is genius—with that and with the dark power that he possessed. But it was fascinating—terrifying and fascinating."

"I should imagine so," said Eddie, wondering by what means he could induce her to forget Michel Benni and his works of darkness. It was as well she was assuming the man to be dead, he reflected, for that would change her outlook, and would leave room for some curative suggestions to be implanted in her mind. "But what about Harold?" he asked. "You say you know that he committed the murder."

"I'm sure of it."

"Does anybody else know?"

"I don't think so."

"But somebody might know?"

"It is possible."

"Then Harold must leave the country. Don't you think so?"

"I suppose that would be advisable."

"And you had better go with him. For one thing, your nerves have been in a pretty bad way lately, and a change will do you good."

Eddie considered that he had been rather wide awake in thus taking advantage of the situation. Whatever the reason, Cynthia was, at the moment, in a normal state of mind; she was free of the influence under which she lately seemed to have been existing, and appeared to be possessed of normally cool judgment. If he could induce her to go abroad for a long holiday, although it might be in the false belief that she was assisting Harry to escape from the law, she would fully recover from the strange effects of her association with Michel Benni. And, what was more important, she would get out of the way of Michel Benni himself.

"Eddie," she said suddenly, "I don't think you believe me when I say that Harold has committed a murder."

"But, my dear—"

"No, you don't!" she cut in, and there was a glint of anger in the look she flashed at him. "I know by your tone. And by your manner. You don't believe me, and you think you'll just humour me. You think I'm imagining things. You're telling yourself that I've had a nervous breakdown and that I'm not responsible for what I say and do. But you're wrong. I only wish you were right."

"My dear girl!" he begged, feeling slightly uncomfortable because he knew that she spoke the truth, and because he was conscious of deserving her reproaches.

"Don't treat me like a child, Eddie," she went on, the glint of anger still persisting. "I telephoned to you to-night because I thought I could rely upon you to believe me. And you assume I am imagining things. You don't credit me with normal sense. You think—"

"Please, Cynthia—" he begged, reaching out a hand and laying it on hers.

"I suppose I can't really expect you to believe me," she said in a quieter voice. "You think that I'm talking rubbish when I maintain, without any practical proof, that Harold killed Michel Benni. But don't think I'm not perfectly well aware of the utter—the utter unreason of it all. Listen, Eddie. I know that Michel Benni is dead. And I know now why I was attracted to him. He could exert some mysterious influence over me. Hypnotism, I think it was. I don't know. I always thought hypnotism meant making passes with the hands, and all that sort of thing. I thought it had all to be prepared beforehand—the patient, or subject, placed in a certain position and told to keep the gaze fixed on some bright object—You know what I mean."

Eddie nodded.

"That, I suppose, is the elementary kind of hypnotism," he said.

"Because there was never anything like that in my case," she went on. "I just gradually felt myself to be in his power. My mind seemed to work in conjunction with his. I knew what he was thinking, and he knew what I was thinking. He seemed to be always present in my life. Can you understand me?"

Eddie nodded. Eddie's expression had become really serious during the past few moments. That is to say, he saw in the affair infinitely more than he had anticipated. This was something more fearful than a breakdown of the nervous system.

"If you have been able to follow me so far," she continued, "you will perhaps be able to believe me when I say again that Michel Benni is dead and that Harold killed him. I was at home this evening. Harold was out. I knew that Michel Benni was at the laboratory in Gurlitt Row. I hadn't been told that he was there; I just knew it, in the same way as I knew lots of things. Then I knew that Harold was there as well. And I knew that Harold intended to kill Michel Benni—to shoot him. He was there a long time and nothing happened. Then, all at once, something did happen. The sense of being in touch with Michel Benni just left me."

She stopped speaking and looked at Eddie as though waiting for his comments.

"And that means—" he began.

"It means that he is dead," she said. "The sense of being in touch with him has never left me for a moment during the past two months. I didn't realize it was that until it suddenly left me tonight. But now I know what it was that attracted me to him. And I'm sure that he's dead."

"I see," said Eddie slowly.

He did not find it hard to believe Cynthia's statements. A few words of explanation had given him the key, and what had seemed hysterical nonsense became grim fact. Then a secondary thought occurred to him.

"But if Michel Benni was as powerful as you say," he remarked, "why didn't he stop Harold?"

Cynthia frowned and shook her head.

"I can't pretend to know that," she answered.

"You say that he knew Harold was going to kill him—or that he was going to try to kill him," Eddie persisted.

"He must have known that, for I knew it," she said. "I couldn't have known it otherwise. I never imagined that Harold would attempt such a thing. I never credited Harold with so much determination. It was the last thing in the world I should have expected to happen, so I wouldn't suddenly become convinced of my own accord that it was actually about to happen. You still don't think it did happen?"

Eddie looked at her across the table, looked very straight into her eyes.

"I'm prepared to believe that it did," he said.

For a few moments they ate in silence.

"So now what can we do?" she asked at length. "To protect Harold, I mean."

"We must find him first. Have you any idea where he might be? Or ought we to go to the laboratory?"

"I don't think we ought to go there," she said. "We don't want to get into the hands of the authorities. We might have to answer such a lot of questions."

"Then where might Harold be?"

"He might be in any of half a dozen places," she replied, searching in her memory. "He's got friends here, there, and everywhere in London."

"Perhaps he'll go home. But perhaps he won't. It depends upon the circumstances. It also depends upon what he imagines you will think about the affair."

"I wish I could locate him," Cynthia murmured wistfully. "He needn't be afraid of what I might think. When I telephoned to you did I say that something dreadful had happened?"

"Those were your words—yes."

"That was only because I was so startled," she said. "But I'm getting a grip on myself now. And I want so much to see Harold. I want so much to see him and tell him that I'll do anything I can for him. I realize now what he has saved me from. And you'll help him too, Eddie, won't you? But of course you will. You won't let him suffer for having killed a man like that."

Eddie hesitated. She thought he was going to argue that deliberate killing was murder, and that one who subscribed to the laws of a country had no right to shield a murderer.

But she got her word in first.

"It isn't murder," she said. "It's killing, but it isn't murder. And though it were," she went on with trembling earnestness, speaking hardly above a whisper on account of the proximity of other diners, "I would still ask for your help. In fact, I should demand it. At the very least I should—"

"My dear girl, have I suggested—"

"Forgive me," she said. "For doubting you, I mean. But you seemed to be hesitating. I wondered whether you had strict ideas about things of that sort. I was ready to be dreadfully disappointed in you. But you wouldn't give Harold away, would you?"

"What I was wondering about, Cynthia," he said, speaking with some diffidence, "was whether Harold would give *you* away. I mean—it might be unfair of me to bring up the old question at this moment, selfishly taking advantage of the situation and all that, but will you marry me? . . . Don't say you would if you would rather not. I can stand another refusal. I've had lots of practice."

And, in the matter of giving refusals, she also had had lots of practice. But in spite of that she seemed to find this one difficult.

"Oh, Eddie," she said, making a futile attempt not to show self-consciousness, "I—I knew I could trust you to do your best for Harold—"

"But that isn't what I asked you," he pointed out.

She was obviously confused. She tried to hide her confusion by adopting a severe attitude.

"A public restaurant is hardly the place for making a proposal," she said. "And the circumstances—yes, it is rather unfair of you to bring up that question now."

"But I've proposed to you in all sorts of places—and in all sorts of circumstances. You have never had any difficulty in declining."

"No, I've never had any difficulty in *declining,*" she said.

CHAPTER X

HAROLD DISCOVERED

KEEP YOUR PLACES!" said Forbes, sharply, breathlessly, as the flat became silent following a startling ring at the door-bell.

Mathers had sprung to his feet. Harringay had half turned in his chair and was staring at the closed door of the sitting-room. Crossland remained still, but his cheeks had changed colour.

The manner of Forbes was not reassuring. It was obvious that Forbes could not immediately put an innocent construction upon that ring at the door-bell. He was searching in his mind, trying to discover there who the ringer might be.

"Keep your places," he repeated in a quieter tone.

He opened the sitting-room door quietly and stood for a moment listening. Then he stepped into the little hall, switching on the light.

Harringay started to talk about the game—started to talk loudly, his remarks punctuated by laughs that sounded disarmingly genuine.

Then they heard the sound of voices coming from the hall. One of them was a woman's voice.

"It's my sister," murmured Harold Crossland, half in alarm.

Mathers, rapidly gathering his wits together, staggered to his feet. He was certainly drunk, although the concentration that had been necessary for poker had kept the fumes of alcohol more or less at bay.

"There's somebody with her. What do they want?" he asked.

Through the minds of the three men there ran convictions that the concealment of the murder had miscarried somewhere. Perhaps Crossland had been seen. Perhaps investigations had been made after the removal of the body by Forbes and Harringay, and some previously-overlooked evidence had come to light.

And none could forget for a moment the horror in the bathroom cupboard.

"What do they want?" Mathers repeated. "I don't like it. I don't like it. We aren't safe yet."

"Shut up!" Harringay hissed, fixing Mathers with a stare that betokened unpleasant things should the young man lose his head. "We're safe as houses—all of us. Only keep your nerve. They can't know anything. Nobody can know anything."

"Wish you'd been able to sink that body in the sea to-night," said Harold Crossland, in the act of listening for any stray words that might penetrate the closed door of the sitting-room.

Harringay brought out an ugly oath. "It'll be in the sea to-morrow night," he snapped.

"Then we can't count ourselves safe till to-morrow night," Mathers retorted.

"And anything might happen before tomorrow night," Harold Crossland put in.

Harringay clenched his right fist.

"His might not be the only body that's dropped overboard," he said, refraining from moving out of his seat as he had seemed to be about to do. "We'd better shuffle again."

A touch at the handle of the door had warned him of a possible influx from the hall. The door opened and Cynthia Crossland stepped into the room, followed by a young man whom Harringay did not know but whom both Crossland and Mathers recognized.

Mathers thought: "What the devil is Landor doing here *to-night?"*

Forbes closed the door. Cynthia started slightly at the sound, but her gaze was fixed on her brother who was now standing at the other side of the table.

"We're sorry to intrude," she said, "but I've been looking all over London for you, Harold. Mr. Forbes tried to tell me that you weren't here, but I happened to hear your voice. If your friends will excuse you—"

Forbes, standing near the door, was trying to catch Harold's eye. To Forbes the principal evil at this stage was that threatened by the emotional states of Crossland and Mathers. These two could not be trusted to act with discretion; the merest suggestion of danger was enough to send them into a panic. He wanted, above all things, to keep them both close to him until the grisly object in the bathroom cupboard should be put completely out of sight.

But Crossland was taking no notice of the attempts to catch his eye. He was begging his sister to permit him to introduce Harringay, and was apparently doing his best to show that he was at least sober. If he had had his wits about him, he must have known that he could not act naturally and that, in the circumstances, it would be as well to make out that he was too drunk to be a desirable companion for the girl. Better to make her leave the place in disgust than let her take her brother off home. Forbes was seething with uncertainty regarding the object of her visit, and should she have learnt that Michel Benni was missing she might easily frighten her brother into making a wild disclosure. However, Crossland was apparently incapable of reasoning these matters out for himself.

"Why didn't you telephone, my dear?" he asked in a conversational tone. "It would have saved you the trouble of looking all over London for me—as you say you've done."

"I should have been told you weren't here," she said, half turning her head and giving Forbes an unmistakably inimical look.

"I owe you a thousand apologies, Miss Crossland," Forbes hastened to say. "I did try to mislead you. I admit it. But please let me explain."

"Perhaps an explanation isn't necessary, Mr. Forbes," she retorted, now looking him fully in the eye.

"What the devil does she mean by that?" Forbes asked himself.

Aloud he said: "Your brother, up to a few minutes ago, seemed too top-heavy to be a suitable companion for a lady. I'm afraid I must admit that the bottle has been circulating pretty freely this evening. And you will understand, Miss Crossland, that I wanted to spare you any distress. However, your appearance seems to have sobered him."

Cynthia let her gaze shift to her brother. Forbes was slightly afraid of her. He was afraid of that penetrating glance of hers and afraid of her general air of self-possession. She seemed to be one who would readily have her suspicions aroused and who would not be easily hoodwinked. And one could not tell what she was thinking.

"I don't know why *my* appearance should sober him," she said.

And again she looked keenly at the two men—her brother and Forbes. It had occurred to her that possibly all these men knew about the murder. She could not guess what interest they might have in the death of Michel Benni, but the atmosphere here was certainly very tense—too tense to be caused by the fear of her discovering that her brother was drunk.

"Isn't there something else, Harold?" she asked, interrupting Harringay who was about to add a few remarks.

Her brother was trying hard to maintain self-control, but when she said that, he could not prevent the blood from seeping from his face.

"I see there is," she said, without giving Harold time to make any answer. "Do these gentlemen also know?"

"Know what?" Forbes asked, alarmed.

"My God!" Mathers said in a choked voice.

"She knows! She knows!" her brother exclaimed, his self-control routed.

Forbes let out an oath.

"Keep quiet!" he barked.

He made no effort to conceal his feelings now. It was obviously futile to pretend that there was nothing the matter. His eyes blazed at Harold, and that had the effect of making the young man remain silent.

"Nobody can know anything," Forbes went on. "It's impossible. Only, rabbits like you rush in and tell everything to the first person who looks at them."

Cynthia stood her ground. Forbes' sudden alteration in manner startled her, certainly, but it was not quite unexpected. She saw that they all knew what had happened; they all knew that Harold had killed Michel Benni, and they were trying to cover him.

But could she be sure of that? Might there not be something else amiss—something else that they wanted to hide? Yes, there was that possibility, unlikely though it might be. And, while the possibility existed, she could not hint at what she knew, for to do so might be to give away Harold's secret to these men—the man Forbes and the man Harringay, neither of whom she could regard but with distrust.

And if they already knew, they would not mention it to her, for they thought it impossible that she should know, and they could not rely upon her to protect even her own brother from the charge of killing the man she was supposed to love.

She must see Harold by himself. "You are coming with me, Harold," she said.

"He's doing nothing of the sort," Forbes answered. "He's staying here."

The law of the jungle was in operation. "He can answer for himself," Eddie Landor said, breaking into the conversation and causing four pairs of eyes to be turned in his direction.

Forbes had been wondering just who this Eddie Landor might be. As a person who lived pretty much on the wrong side of the law, Forbes was naturally suspicious of anyone who looked upright, and the fair-haired young man had the manner of one who would do the honourable thing in any circumstances. And the honourable thing in Landor's estimation might not be very acceptable to Forbes.

Eddie looked at the four men—one after another. There could hardly be a doubt that what Cynthia so mysteriously knew had actually taken place, and there could hardly be a doubt that these men knew all about it. But Eddie, like Cynthia, could not be absolutely sure on that point, and it was not for him to lay the cards on the table. In silence they looked at him and he looked at them; then the silence was broken by the high-pitched "brrr" of the door-bell.

CHAPTER XI

THE INTRUDERS

THE START Cynthia gave was not unnoticed by the four conspirators. But for that they might have suspected that here was someone else calling by arrangement to support her in her wish to take her brother away; and in that case they might have imagined that she had found out about the misuse of her money and that she was going to get the truth from Harold before she started proceedings.

But when the bell rang, a look that was very decidedly a look of alarm crossed her face. Forbes wondered at that. He hesitated for an instant, not knowing how to act; but quickly he decided upon acting as disarmingly as possible. It was one thing to permit the girl to believe that they did not want her to have the opportunity of cross-questioning her brother; it was something quite different to give the impression that they were afraid to allow anyone into the flat, for that would be to raise the suspicion that the flat itself held something that was to be concealed. And to raise that suspicion would be to cause the girl to make enquiries. To Forbes she seemed that sort of girl, and he did not know whether she suspected that something had happened to Michel Benni.

With a muttered word of excuse, he went out into the hall and opened the outer door.

Two men stood there. They were not of the type who rang Forbes' bell in the ordinary way, and Forbes was not only surprised but was decidedly uneasy to see them there. On this night every unusual circumstance was suspect, and these two men were suspect even before they opened their mouths to state their business.

Both were big men, and they had about them that air of freshness and cleanliness that goes hand in hand with a Sunday suit. They were obviously not gentlemen—assuming Forbes to be a gentleman—and that fact added to Forbes' uneasiness.

"Begging your pardon, sir," said one of the men—a red-faced individual with the physique of a bricklayer—"but we're looking for some friends of a Mr. Benni—"

"Professor Benni," interposed the other.

"Professor Benni," said the first, "which lives in this here building. We thought—"

"Nobody of the name of Professor Benni lives in this building," said Forbes, now decidedly uneasy, but trusting to his nimbleness of wit and his generally imposing manner to stave off this strange pair.

"You don't know the name, sir?" the bricklayer fellow asked.

Forbes noticed the wistfulness of the fellow's tone. What the fellow wanted he could not guess, and for the moment he was too greatly concerned with the business of getting rid of the two callers to try to account for their presence. His darting thoughts took account only of the men's manner. Their disappointment at being informed that Michel Benni did not live there showed how simply they could be handled.

"No," Forbes told them, with an air of regret, "I don't know anybody of the name of—what did you say?—Benni. Perhaps if you try some of the other flats—"

"This is where we does our stuff, 'Arry," said the bricklayer, cutting short Forbes' words and stepping briskly into the flat. "We just wanted you to say that, see!" he explained, pushing his face close to Forbes'. "That's what we wanted you to say—that you didn't know 'im, see! 'For why?' says you. Well, I don't mind tellin' you for why. It's just because you said—"

"Don't jaw so much, Alf," said his companion. "While you're jawin' he's makin' up his mind what to say."

"It don't matter how much the bloke makes up 'is mind," Alf retorted. "He don't get away with it now. Not now that he's said he don't know the Professor, see!"

By this time both men were in the hall, and Harry, who was also of the labourer type, had closed the door.

Forbes tried to protest, but the men—hulking beings who were careless of the finer points of etiquette—simply brushed aside his protests by the sheer force of their physical might.

"Harringay!" Forbes called, and the word was like a staccato cry that expressed fear as well as a sense of outrage.

In an instant Harringay was in the hall.

"What's the matter?"

"Oh, here's the other bloke!" Alf the bricklayer said, speaking as though he were, on the whole, pleased to have Harringay brought into the affair. "This is a bit of luck, this is. Maybe *you* don't happen to know a gentleman of the name of Benni—

Professor Benni?" he asked, staring very threateningly at Harringay.

"Well, it don't matter," said his companion. "We know just where we stand, so it don't matter what the bloke says about it."

Forbes, despite the confident manner of the intruders, stepped towards the telephone and put his hand on the receiver.

"If you aren't out of here in ten seconds," he said, "I'll dial the police."

"Dial away, old cock!" said Alf.

"We'll help you, if you like," said his companion.

"What do they want?" Harringay asked. Harringay had gone rather white about the gills.

"What do we want!" Alf echoed.

"I'll tell you what we want," his companion interposed. "We want that case what you took from Professor Benni's place. That's what we want. The case—*and* the contents."

"But this is outrageous," Forbes blurted out.

"The case we took from Professor Benni's place?" said Harringay. "What right have you to come here demanding—"

"As much right as you had to take it," said Alf.

"But Professor Benni told us to go and get it," Harringay stated firmly. "What has it got to do with you? Who are you anyway?"

"Oh, Professor Benni told you to go and get it, did he?" Alf retorted. "Well, that's a queer thing, that is. Your pal here says he don't know nobody of the name of Professor Benni. That's what he said, 'Arry, ain't it?"

"That's what he said, all right," his companion agreed.

"We caught 'im, see!" said Alf. "We says, innocent like, 'Happen to know, sir, if any friends of Professor Benni's live here?' we says; and your pal he looks like he was considering, then he says, 'Sorry, you fellers, but I don't know nobody of that name. I would try some of the other flats if I was you,' he says,"

"Well, what about it?" Harringay asked, while fear gripped his throat.

"Just this," said Alf. "He told my old mother only to-night that Professor Benni had sent him and you to bring away a case of chemicals. That's what about it. And now he says he don't know Professor Benni. So that shows. My old mother she thought it looked a bit fishy, but she didn't like to say nothin'. Only, she sent my little brother to follow you on 'is bike. Then when I comes home she says, 'You go and see what's what,' she says. 'Looks fishy to me,' she says. And sure enough it does look fishy all right. So what about that case—*and* the contents?"

"But, my dear man—" said Forbes who, in spite of the disastrous turn of events, seemed still to have hopes of warding off evil.

"We don't want no soft soap," Alf warned him. "We want that there case."

"But Professor Benni knows we have it," Harringay interposed. "I can't understand—"

"You see," said Forbes, cursing this unexpected accident that might put a noose round the neck of every man concerned, "I didn't know who you were. It's all right for Professor Benni, but it doesn't follow that I'm compelled to answer your question truthfully. In fact, I was justified in speaking as I did, for Michel Benni himself told us not to let on where the case was. It is concerned with one of his experiments, which are of a very-secret nature. I'm telling you this because you seem to be, in a manner, justified in making enquiries. I take it that his possessions are more or less in your care when he is away from the place, and I commend your eagerness in looking after his interests. But in this case, I assure you that he will be very much annoyed if your eagerness spoils the experiment that is at present going on. You seem to be men of sense, so you will understand—"

"Soft soap!" Alf murmured, and took a couple of heavy strides further into the hall, stopping with his hand on the nearest door, which was that leading to Forbes' bedroom.

Forbes darted back to the telephone, from which he had wandered during the course of his last remarks.

"Look here!" he exclaimed. "You've no right to come in here and do what you like. Even the police haven't the right to do that without a search-warrant."

"That's just it," said Alf. "If they had we'd 'uv brought them along. But we can do what the police can't do, see! The police must act official. We don't have to. 'Arry, you stand by that telephone, and if the gentlemen kicks up rough you dial 999. We know when the police is wanted and when they ain't wanted."

Without further remark he opened the door of the bedroom and switched on the light.

Forbes did not waste time in further protest of a mild order. He knew that argument was useless. But at all costs they must prevent the discovery of what the bathroom held, and the only way of preventing that discovery was by the use of force. Harringay, he saw, was edging towards the telephone. Harringay's intention was obviously to settle the man who stood there ready to bring the police. He himself flung open the door of the sitting-room. The three men and the girl were standing in attitudes of expectancy, and at his appearance they stepped forward.

The fellow Landor was the only one who could be relied upon to be of much use. Crossland seemed to lack stamina. Mathers was a weakling and, at the moment, was further handicapped by being unsteady on his feet. Forbes tried to estimate his own ability when it should come to a fight, and had to admit that the two intruders gave him no room to hope that he might be of much use. He was short and they were bulky, and though he was wiry his wiriness would not stand him in very good stead in the present case, for these two men would simply slash out with sledge-hammer blows. Harringay was the only one who could be accounted a match for them.

And faith in Harringay was quickly dispersed. The man guarding the telephone, seeing that Harringay was about to take action, shot out a mighty fist and Harringay dropped to his knees. Good living was no adequate preparation for meeting violence of this sort.

Harold Crossland and Eddie rushed forward, but Forbes stepped in front of them and kept them back.

"Stop!" he cried. "That's no good. You'll make these men imagine that we have something to hide, and we haven't anything to hide. I don't mind their looking over the place, so far as my conscience is concerned. I only resent it as an unwarrantable intrusion. I am thinking mainly of the Professor's experiment—"

While he was speaking, he was assisting Harringay to his feet. He was also cursing the luck that had induced that old woman to become suspicious. The irony of it! Little did she think that in busying herself with reclaiming stolen property she was about to unearth a murder!

And there was no way of avoiding it.

The man who had gone into the bedroom now returned and strode towards the bathroom. Forbes flew at him. Forbes simply lost his head and did the instinctive thing. In another moment he had been felled with a single blow.

"Dial 999," said Alf to his companion, as Eddie rushed at him.

Harringay caught Eddie round the waist. "Don't do that," he said to the man at the telephone.

Cynthia could not quite grasp the significance of what was happening, but she could at least gather that her brother was in danger. Harold's murder of Michel Benni was the supreme matter of the moment, and any unusual happening must have reference to that, she was convinced.

The man, Alf, opened the bathroom door and switched on the light. Harold Crossland and Mathers made a rush at him; but among these men who led indolent lives he was utterly invincible. He did not deign to hit Mathers; he gripped him by the shoulder and flung him back into the hall, then stepped into the bathroom and stood looking round.

Naturally, the cupboard was the first thing to attract his attention.

Forbes, struggling to his feet, heard a grunt of satisfaction that was immediately followed by a violent oath.

"Stop him!" he cried. "Stop him! Why don't you stop him?"

Eddie Landor, who had only the faintest notion of what the whole affair was about—for he never dreamt that the body of Michel Benni was in this flat—jumped into the bathroom automatically in response to Forbes' words. He remembered seeing Harold Crossland and Mathers shrinking, white-faced, against the wall, close to where Cynthia stood. He saw Harringay looking quickly and fearfully from the man at the telephone to the open door of the bathroom. He saw Forbes struggling to his feet.

Then he saw the face of the big labourer fellow who seemed to be the chief cause of this disturbance. The man's face was grey, whereas it had been of a healthy red due to much exposure to the weather. And he was looking fearfully out into the hall, then down into the corner of the bathroom.

Eddie, too, looked down into the corner, where a cupboard door stood open, disclosing a large box. The lid of the box lay on the floor. In a heap on top of it lay a white sheet or garment. And a single glance told Eddie that that sheet had covered the body of Michel Benni.

Alf sprang to life and dragged the box out on to the floor. At the same time he called to his companion to ring for the police.

"999," he shouted. "And tell them it's murder. And bash anybody that tries to get away. No, wait a minute—wait a minute!"

Cynthia had screamed on hearing the mention of murder, and now she was holding on to the doorpost of the sitting-room for support. Mathers was looking, panic-stricken, towards the bedroom, from the window of which a fire escape led down to the ground. A revolver had appeared in Harold Crossland's hand, and he might have been contemplating two more murders as a means of covering up his first.

But the suddenly altered tone of the man who had made the discovery in the bathroom arrested everybody's attention.

It was Eddie who saw the reason for that altered tone.

And the reason—to Eddie—was simple enough. To Harold Crossland, who now staggered into the bathroom, the reason was terrifying in the extreme. He felt himself to be trembling.

The body of Michel Benni was moving. The man was not dead. The shoulders heaved slowly, the fingers of one hand twitched. And presently the eyelids began to flicker with little nervous impulses.

Eddie breathed a sigh of relief. But Harold Crossland could only stare, wide-eyed. Harold, who ought to have seen in the movements of the body his own reprieve from the hands of the hangman, experienced not relief but fear—a strange fear. A thousand thoughts flashed through his mind—thoughts mainly of the kind to induce terror. It was perhaps possible for a man with two bullets in his chest to live, but Harold did not regard those flickering eyelids and those heaving shoulders as indicating that the bullets had taken freakish paths and that, by one chance in a million, they had failed to touch a vital spot. Had he thought so he would have felt a sense of relief as profound as that felt by Eddie. But his feeling was one of terror in the face of dark mystery. "Give us a hand," Alf shouted.

CHAPTER XII

STRANGE SAYINGS

THE BULKY FIGURE of Michel Benni stood swaying on its feet, and the group just within the bathroom doorway stared.

"May I—may I beg a sip of brandy?" Michel Benni murmurmured.

Forbes, walking backwards and not taking his gaze from the man who had thus returned to life, moved to the sitting-room door. Michel Benni smiled, while supporting himself on the arm of Alf. Then, making an effort at regaining his strength, he stepped slowly forward in the wake of Forbes.

The persons in his path drew aside as they might from some grisly spectacle that engendered fear and at the same time fascination. No one spoke. Michel Benni moved slowly, with an occasional pause as though for breath, towards the door of the sitting-room.

"I can manage now," he said to Alf, disengaging himself from the bricklayer's sturdy hold. "I am much obliged to you, Alfred."

Alf and his companion remained uncertainly in the hall. They did not know the meaning of these strange occurrences, and particularly they could not account for the frightened faces of the other persons present; but they assumed that the gentleman had been speaking the truth when he said that the Professor was trying some experiment or other. Here was the experiment and they had blundered into it, and it was no wonder that the gentleman had been excited and all scared-like, for experiments of this sort might be touchy things that it wouldn't take much to upset.

Without too much fuss the two men withdrew from the flat, feeling that they had made fools of themselves for interfering in affairs that were, after all, no concern of theirs.

The rest of those present moved into the sitting-room, drawn there by fearful curiosity.

Michel Benni was seated at the table which, with its complement of the sideboard, made the room a dining-room as well. His cheeks now had almost their normal colour and his manner was already that of a man who was in good health. The fire had come back to his eyes. He looked round the group.

"You are all present, I see," he said. "And you too, my dear," he added, allowing his glance to rest for a moment on Cynthia. "That is good, and I thank you for assisting so admirably in this experiment. You, my dear Harold, I thank particularly for doing what I might not have had the courage to do by myself. You see, I did tell you, did I not, that I proposed carrying out an interesting experiment to-night? I begged of you to assist me. You were, however, so ungracious as to refuse your assistance. Nevertheless, you did assist me. And, if I am any judge, I think you find the experiment interesting—as I said you would. The interest is all-absorbing, is it not? Nothing that you have ever dabbled in has been so engrossing as this. Am I not right?"

Harold Crossland did not answer. He and the rest could only stare.

Michel Benni was smiling, but it was a grim kind of smile that belied the pleasant manner in which he spoke.

"Yes, I have to thank you," he went on. "Without your assistance I might not, as I say, have had the courage to perform the experiment. Not, of course, that I can give you credit for being anything more than an unwitting assistant. In fact, I could very well have you handed over to the authorities on a charge of attempted murder—you and your three friends." He glanced at Harringay, Forbes and Mathers in turn, and his smile became still more grim. "Not that I will do so," he said. "I can manage these things so much better by myself."

A chilly fear gripped the hearts of those present. The sight of this man sitting there after having been shot twice through the chest was sufficiently amazing in all conscience, for even assuming that the bullets had, by a million-to-one chance, failed to be almost immediately fatal, they could not fail to have a disabling effect. No normal man could withstand that effect, but Michel Benni was withstanding it.

Harringay, recovering somewhat, glanced at Forbes. Harringay was thinking of Harold Crossland's eagerness to know that the body was sunk deep in the ocean. Crossland's fears, it seemed, had not been exaggerated. He had said that he was afraid of the body—that he thought the body might bring disaster upon them. And Forbes had scoffed at the notion. But perhaps Forbes was now thinking differently about Crossland's queer intuition.

Intuition—that was it. Harringay had been affected by it, too. He had been inclined to believe that Crossland was not talking merely in a hysterical way, but that he had some strange faith in his own statements. And Crossland had been right. The dead body had indeed been something to fear, for the dead body had come to life again. He could not imagine this to be a case of a couple of freakish shots that had done no damage—even if that were a possibility. There was something abnormal about the *man* rather than about the *occurrence.* Abnormal, or supernatural . . . His remarks about an experiment showed that the awakening was not accidental. It was in accordance with his own expectations. And now he was saying that he would not take any legal action in the matter, that he could manage these things so much better by himself.

"You see, my dear Harold," the man went on, "I warned you of the folly of remaining in ignorance of the strength of your opponent. Had you taken my warning, you would first of all have assured yourself that you and a revolver, together, were stronger than I. You imagine that it was impossible for you to decide that point. But think, my dear Harold. I dealt very fairly with you. When you presented yourself at my laboratory I did not conceal from you the fact that I was aware of your intentions. For I was aware of them, I assure you. I knew your thoughts. I have not lived for over four hundred years—lived and thought and studied—without acquiring a higher degree of mental development than is possible in the case of a man who fives only the normal span."

He paused as his listeners all started simultaneously—he paused and looked round the group and smiled at their expressions which were half of fear and half of incredulity.

"And why should I not have lived for over four hundred years?" he asked. "There is nothing of wizardry in that. I only ask you to consider your present-day scientists. You do not think they are mad when they experiment with the object of discovering a means whereby the effects of age might be counteracted. One of your present-day scientists has, indeed, made some advances in that direction. But when he meets with some success you do not say that he is in league with the devil. You accept his success as a normal development of science. So why should you be amazed—and afraid—when I tell you that I have lived for over four hundred years? It is merely that I discovered the secret of arresting the effects of age before anyone else discovered it. And, given that discovery, time is of no consequence. As you see me now, so I have remained throughout four centuries—a man who is apparently of about fifty years of age.

"I have imparted my secret to no one. There has been no need for me to hurry. Time, as I say, is of no consequence. In the meantime I have been working to discover a method whereby I might guard against—accidents. For the ability to counteract the ravages of time is not enough. Death comes by other ways than old age. Diseases, for instance. Or poisons. Or *bullets*.

"Now, with so much time at my disposal, it was inevitable that I should eventually succeed in my researches, if success were possible. And success is assuredly possible. I paid particular attention to the self-healing virtues in animal tissue, believing that these virtues could be developed far beyond their natural capacity, although their natural capacity is amazing in certain instances; a savage warrior will, in a day or two, recover from an axe blow that would kill a white man on the spot, and some of the lowest members of the animal world grow new limbs when the old limbs have been accidentally severed.

"My experiment to-night has completely assured me that I have succeeded in making myself impervious to the effects of bullets. I was already assured that no poison could harm me. As for the risk of being smothered! That is nothing. Even the Indian sorcerers—so called—can avoid that, as you know, for they allow themselves to be buried in the ground for weeks on end, and are found to be still alive when they are dug up again.

"Now, perhaps, you guess why I trouble to tell you all this," he continued, after glancing keenly at the faces of his audience of six. "You guess, perhaps?"

Forbes shot a look at Harringay. Harringay met the look, but met it blankly. These men, adepts at giving signs, had nothing to say to each other. They were aware only of impending discomfort or worse. The manner of Michel Benni was suave and pleasant, but it was the manner of one who is conscious of his power and who might show his fangs at *any* moment. For the present he was warning them against making any further attempt on his life.

A new kind of fear gripped Forbes. That the man was speaking the truth he had no doubt. Hence his fear—a kind of fear he had never experienced except in nightmare. A man whom you could not kill! He savoured the fear keenly. He imagined himself with his fingers about that throat, pressing the windpipe with his whole strength, pressing till the muscles of his fingers ached so that he could hold on no longer; and the man would not be dead. He imagined himself shooting, shooting, shooting—emptying a revolver into that body—and the horror of seeing that the shots were taking no effect. Wild thoughts of that sort surged through his brain. He did not reckon upon the fact that the man had remained inert for some hours after the shots were fired by Crossland. Possibly the next time he would never lose consciousness. This present case was in the nature of an experiment, and no doubt the man had learnt something from it. He would not again put himself at their mercy.

"No," said Michel Benni, looking up at Forbes as though Forbes had spoken aloud, "I shall not again put myself at your mercy. In any case, you will not again make an attempt upon my life. You see, I am being quite frank with you. I have been very frank with you throughout. I have explained my re-awakening to life, and that I would not explain to any but a selected few, for I still wish to keep my knowledge secret. And now you probably ask why I regard you people selected few worthy of hearing what I have told you?"

CHAPTER XIII

SENTENCE

"WELL, GENTLEMEN—" Michel Benni continued; then he paused and turned towards Cynthia. "I exclude you, my dear," he murmured, "in what I am about to say."

Cynthia was standing grasping Eddie by the sleeve of his coat. Her eyes, like those of the others, were staring at the speaker. She took no apparent notice of his reference to herself, but simply continued to stare.

"I should not care, gentlemen," he went on, "for the publicity that would be given to me should it become known that I had discovered the secret of indefinitely continued life. That would interfere with my plans. I tell it to you, however, for several reasons. For one thing, I do not wish to be put to any inconvenience through your making another attempt to kill me. I want you to understand that such an attempt would be quite futile; and though you would not be able to make it while I prohibited it, you might take me off my guard for a moment. In such a case you might be arrested for attempted murder, and I do not wish you to get into the hands of the authorities. No, I do not wish you to—get into the hands of the authorities."

The curious way in which he said that brought a number of involuntary movements from his spellbound listeners. Cynthia turned her head slowly and glanced at the faces of the four who stood a little apart—her brother, Forbes, Mathers, and Harringay. Their gaze was fixed on the face of Michel Benni. She glanced up at Eddie, feeling herself to be clutching his arm with all the force at her command. He did not notice her glance; he, too, was gazing fixedly at the face of the man who sat at the table.

It was as though they were all fascinated to the extent of being utterly unaware of anything except the man addressing them.

"I tell you these things for another reason," Michel Benni went on. "It gives me pleasure to do so. That is another reason. And I may do so with safety, knowing that you will never divulge my secret to anyone. Should you try to do so—to tell that you have found a man who stopped ageing four hundred years ago—the words will die in your throats. You may ask why it should give me pleasure to tell you all about myself. Let me give you the reason.

"In four hundred years one sees much and tastes many pleasures. The things that were wont to stir the emotions lose their interest, for use blunts the capacity for enjoyment. And so life becomes—or can become—an intolerable burden. The essence of enjoyment is interest, and the essence of interest is novelty. The only novelty left to one who has lived as long as I is the novelty to be got from mental development. The pleasures of the senses remain the same or they may decline. The body remains the same. The world remains essentially the same. Only the mind is capable of development, and the mind, year by year, becomes keener and keener, knows more and more; that is why I possess powers of which you have no conception. Life to you is seventy steps forward and sixty-nine steps back. To me it is four hundred steps forward. The difference is too great to be reckoned in terms of mental accomplishment; you are still children awaking in a bright, new world and wondering at the meaning of what you see about you.

"But to me all that is stale—all *except* a few emotions. I have not, for instance, indulged overmuch in the pleasure of killing. I have killed a number of men in my time, but not so many as to make me wholly indifferent to the knowledge that I have caused a man to die. I can still derive a certain pleasure from that. And it occurs to me that here is an opportunity for a little amusement.

"Not merely amusement, of course! Always when I meet people who are troublesome to me I kill them. It is so easy to kill them. And it is something to have the sense of power. It is also amusing to decide the manner of their deaths. Of course, I do not use daggers and guns. The pleasure of these crude methods of administering death is satisfactory only to children, who have their emotions stirred by the mere act of extinguishing a life. To me, with so much power at my command, some amusement is to be derived from trying to discover novel ways of killing.

"Let me see. There are four of you. No, five of you," he corrected himself, with a glance at Eddie Landor. "You, young man," he went on, addressing Eddie, "had the rashness to try to discover why Miss Crossland preferred me to you. In your mind you suspected her of madness and me of being the cause. You wondered how you might destroy my influence over her. I gave you one warning, but you were so foolish as to ignore it. I caused you to imagine that I was standing on the doorstep with you when you were paying the lady a midnight call. That was a simple trick, I admit—a trick so simple that it can be learnt during one short lifetime and is used by the more advanced of the Indian mystics. They call it mass-hypnotism, and by its means they make persons see strange things happening when, in actuality, nothing is happening at all.

"Be that as it may, you chose to ignore the warning. You tell yourself that you are determined to destroy the association that exists between Miss Crossland and myself. You have, in fact, asked her to marry you—so her thoughts tell me—and she, imagining me to be dead, consented. But I have chosen her for a mightier part than that of an ordinary man's wife. Let me explain."

Not one word had been spoken by any of the others since Michel Benni started to address them. And no one spoke now. All heard him with an attention that might have indicated respect had it not been for their staring eyes. These indicated fear—and helplessness in the face of that fear. And in the case of Eddie Landor, Forbes and Harringay, at least, their unwavering attention indicated some mysterious compulsion to listen, for they were not of the type that hears its own doom without protest.

Michel Benni, perceiving the continued silence, smiled.

"Miss Crossland will put herself unreservedly into my hands," he went on. "It is fortunate that I met such a charming young lady just at this stage of my career, for I have now formed the intention of putting my powers to their full use. That is to say, I shall found a race of beings who will have my own capacity for continued existence. In a year, at most, Miss Crossland will belong to the company of those who will never die. The process of inoculation will take that length of time. Thereafter she will never grow a day older in appearance; she will grow older only in wisdom. And she and I will found a race of the undying—a race that will multiply and multiply and cover the face of the earth, that will exterminate those who are born to live only for an allotted span, and that will know no law save my commands . . . And you, my dear—"

He rose and took a step towards Cynthia, one hand extended as though to take her arm.

But Cynthia, with a choked cry, moved quickly back.

"No!" she screamed. "Oh, please, no! I should go mad. I should go mad. To live on and on—"

Eddie stepped in front of her and stood in the path of Michel Benni. In a flash he saw the horror of eternal life. It had been sought by the old alchemists as the thing most to be desired in creation, but he was sure that none of them had paused to consider the fearfulness of the condition at which they aimed. To live for ever! To taste all experiences for the sake of making existence bearable, to become weary and ever more weary of life, and gradually to go insane because the human mind was not capable of supporting an existence that had no end!

For a moment Eddie felt that he could defy this wizard who could defy death. The thought of Cynthia gave him strength. Cynthia had promised to be his wife, and that was enough to give a man the power to overcome any evil.

But Michel Benni only smiled at his attitude of defiance.

Then Cynthia stepped slowly forward, passing him and moving towards the smiling, self-confident wizard. She raised her hand a little way. He grasped it and bowed over it, lifting it to his lips. Cynthia stood upright, twisting her body slightly as though the touch of the man's lips on her hand was physically painful. And Eddie had not the will to make one move.

But within him there burned such a fierce desire to destroy the man who was bringing chaos into the world, and who was condemning Cynthia to an eternity of horror that it required no very extraordinary powers to read his thoughts. They blazed in his eyes. But he could not move so that he might act in accordance with his thoughts. His limbs seemed to be paralysed, as did the limbs of the other men.

"Let me take you home, my dear," Michel Benni said. "I need spend no further time on these gentlemen for the present. I shall consider them later—one by one. It will afford me some amusement to do so. One by one. That is a good thought. It will provide quite a lengthy entertainment."

He moved towards the door, half a pace behind Cynthia, who walked slowly with her gaze to the floor.

At the door he turned, and there was a gleam of enthusiasm in his eyes.

"It has just occurred to me," he said, "that you, Harold, ought to be hanged, if you subscribe to the laws of your country. You are virtually a murderer. So what more fitting than that you should indeed be hanged—for murder? I have thought of something that, as you will no doubt agree, is a perfect piece of artistry. If you were to kill our friend who had the rashness to propose marriage to your sister, that would dispose of him. And it would also dispose of you in a very proper manner . . . You must agree that that is an artistically perfect notion! I must consider it more fully. All in good time."

He bowed to the transfixed group, then turned and accompanied Cynthia from the room.

The five men remained motionless until long after the latch of the outer door clicked. Then the restraining influence seemed to be withdrawn from them all simultaneously.

Mathers staggered towards the sideboard. Harringay and Forbes turned and looked blankly at each other.

"I knew it! I knew it!" exclaimed Harold Crossland. "I told you—"

"Shut up, Harold!" said Eddie Landor. "Do you mean to say that five of us can't settle *him?*"

His words and tone were in the highest degree confident, but having spoken he stood biting his lip, while a troubled frown crossed his face.

CHAPTER XIV

MATHERS

MATHERS LEFT the flat in Regent Street and turned down in the direction of Piccadilly Circus. Crossland had already gone, accompanied by that fellow Landor, to see whether Cynthia had reached home safely. That had left only Harringay and Forbes in the flat, and Mathers had felt frozen out.

He knew that he would never have been let in on this deal with Cynthia's money if he had not, at the time, been on the point of becoming engaged to Cynthia. They had wanted him neither for his brains nor for his ability to carry through a swindle. They had taken him into their confidence only because they expected him soon to be in a position from which he could blow their schemes sky-high should he choose, for as Cynthia's husband he would soon have some knowledge of Cynthia's financial affairs. Then she had thrown him over. He had not really been surprised at that. In fact, had he expected the case to be otherwise he would almost certainly have refused to fall in with the scheme for speedily acquiring riches in spite of the convincing way that Forbes had presented the scheme.

But, in any case, that was all over, and he knew that both Harringay and Forbes regarded him as a dead weight in their operations, for he was taking a fourth of the profits and was doing nothing in exchange.

Mathers, as he walked down Regent Street, had the sleekness of a tiger; but his thoughts showed that he had the soul of a rat. He was somewhat dazed by all that had happened that evening, but he was not so dazed as to fail to realize that he himself had not raised a hand against Michel Benni. Crossland had been right when he had said, as they left the flat on the previous night, that he, Mathers, would have backed out had the cards indicated him as the one to commit the murder. Yes, he would have backed out.

Why not? Crossland, too, might have backed out. Nobody could have *forced* him to shoot the man even though the cut of the cards did indicate him. Honour? To Hades with honour!

Of course, had he backed out they would have regarded him with scorn. He would have been ostracized. But what of it? It would certainly have meant a few moments of extreme discomfort. Perhaps they would have given him a thrashing, with a view to teaching him what honour meant. But he would have got over that.

However, he had been lucky. The cards had been kind, and the job had not fallen to him. He had not even assisted in removing the body from the place in Gurlitt Row. He had done nothing.

And now it occurred to him that that fact might be turned to account. He could not doubt that Michel Benni meant what he had said. The very thought of the man sent a cold shiver down Mather's back. Mathers had never been so profoundly terrified in his life. He was more or less sober now, but he was still a little dazed, and had some difficulty in sorting out the events of the evening. Some of them had seemed to be fantastic. But his deep feeling of dread was real enough. It amounted to something like nightmare. That was it—nightmare. He was now in Piccadilly Circus, but it was not the Piccadilly Circus that he knew so well. The fights were possibly as dazzling, and the near-midnight crowds were no doubt animated by the same sense of irresponsibility; but he himself could get no thrill out of the garishness.

It never occurred to him to doubt the statements of Michel Benni. The man had convinced by something other than reason. You felt his power. And, feeling that power, you realized that the world was not as you had thought it to be. The sense of security faded away, and all that had been familiar was shown to be emptiness. Reality was something terrifying, something that the ordinary mortal could not grasp. Reality was in the mind and not in things like trees and houses and people. And the ordinary mortal knew nothing of this reality. A few of the philosophers had sensed it, but nothing more.

Try as he might, Mathers could not shake off the feeling of horror that had descended upon him with the realization of the existence of hitherto unsuspected forces. The man, Michel Benni, carried with him the power of life and death—a strange power against which there seemed to be no safeguard. That was it—against which there seemed to be no safeguard.

There had been five men in that room listening to their death sentence, and they had been unable to raise a hand to defend themselves. Michel Benni's power extended to the physical control of others; he could will a man to act or not to act and the man had to obey. Had Mathers not felt the restriction that had been mysteriously placed upon his muscles in that room, he might have doubted some of the man's statements, particularly the statement that the five of them would presently die—one after another.

But he had to credit the man with the powers he claimed to possess.

And he did not want to die. Not even to die naturally. For a doctor to pronounce the death sentence would be bad enough. To be given a year to live, to know that an incurable malady was gradually gaining ground and that in a year death would supervene—though it might be a painless death—that would be a condition that might make the stoutest heart quail. And this was infinitely worse. To be the plaything of a madman, to be like a brute doomed to slaughter for the amusement of the heartless—a brute that cannot match cunning with cunning, but can only defend itself after the manner of its kind! To know that at that moment, perhaps, Michel Benni was engaged in the diversion of deciding how the deaths might be brought about!

Mathers was standing on the edge of the pavement watching the traffic almost without seeing it. It was the hour at which the theatres emptied themselves. The place was a jumble of taxis, cars and buses, all eager with impatience. It struck him that it would be a simple matter to step off the pavement in front of a lumbering bus. How many tons did a bus weigh? But could he be sure of being killed? Perhaps he would only be mutilated and condemned to weeks or months of frightful pain. And, anyway, why think of suicide?

Mathers laughed, though feeling no sense of amusement. He laughed at the incongruity of his thoughts. To kill oneself in order to save oneself from being killed was a strange way of managing matters.

A taxi shot past within inches of him as he stood there on the edge of the pavement. He drew back with a little exclamation of alarm. He felt his heart to be beating with throbs that shook his body.

"You won't kill me that way!" he exclaimed under his breath, addressing the absent Michel Benni and withdrawing quickly into the crowd and pushing his way to the inner side of the pavement.

The fact that he could do this gave him some confidence. He was sure that the wizard had been turning him towards the contemplation of suicide, and had he given way to the influence of his thoughts he might readily have stepped off the edge of the pavement into the swarm of vehicles.

But he had been granted a certain control over his actions. He could withdraw to the inner side of the pavement. He stood leaning against a corner of Swan & Edgar's premises and congratulated himself upon not letting the thought of suicide take too firm a hold on his mind.

Possibly he had the power to defy Michel Benni. Possibly if he took care not to let his mind drift towards thoughts of death he would be able to escape the sentence. He saw how Michel Benni's power might work. The wizard—the madman—could undoubtedly influence one's thoughts if one were not on the alert. Some kind of telepathy could be brought into play, and if the proposed victim did not rigorously keep his mind under control it would begin to give way to the suggestions offered to it. It might be suggested that deliberate suicide would be better than existing in fear of death, and so the proposed victim would, of his own wish apparently, execute the threat of the wizard.

Having stood leaning against the corner of Swan & Edgar's premises for some minutes, Mathers decided to move on. He was hesitating over a line of action that might possibly be to his advantage. He had been thinking about it ever since leaving Forbes' flat, but as it meant coming face to face again with Michel Benni, it required some consideration. He was wondering whether he dared go to the laboratory and see Michel Benni and tell him all he knew about the affair. The wisdom of such a course would depend, however, upon whether the man had the power to read people's thoughts without hindrance. In such a case he would already know everything that was to be known, including the fact that the four men who had conspired to kill him had been illegally making use of Cynthia Crossland's money. But if he did not know that, he might be pleased to have the information given to him so that he could take steps to get possession of the fortune; for it was to be assumed that even he could make use of money.

At the same time Mathers could point out that he himself had no share in the attempted murder, that he would not have tried to commit the murder even though the lot had fallen to him, and that, so far as the shooting was concerned, only Crossland, Harringay and Forbes were really guilty.

Yes, to go and put the facts before Michel Benni might be a wise move. It might placate him. It would make him all the more eager to execute his threat in the case of the other three, anyway, and there was just the chance that it might make him look with favour upon the informant, Mathers himself.

Yet, it required courage to go to that laboratory.

Still trying to come to a decision, he left the shelter of Swan & Edgar's and strolled off. He neither knew nor cared much in which direction he was going; he only felt the need for being on the move. And if he were keenly on the alert so as not to risk his life in the traffic, he could hardly come to any harm. His chief concern was to obey the traffic fights. And presently walking might help him to come to a decision about the advisability of becoming king's evidence.

In due course he found himself on the Embankment, and was surprised that he should have walked so far without having noticed where he was going. But the place did not matter; so far as he was concerned he desired only to keep on the move. He was less conscious of the overpowering personality of Michel Benni while he was active. The thought of going home and going to sleep brought with it profound foreboding. To sleep would be to leave his mind at the mercy of such fearful influences as Michel Benni could evoke. Yet, one could not walk about for ever.

Then he remembered that there were tram-cars that ran underground from the Embankment to Bloomsbury. Could he assume that his having accidentally wandered to this part of London was an indication that he should go to Bloomsbury and to the laboratory and make his own case good?

The wide pavement flanked by the river wall was deserted mainly. Here and there, at tramcar stopping points, a group of persons would stand shivering with the cold; and here and there on the benches an outcast wretch would sit, shoulders hunched and face hidden as well as coat collar could hide it. The white glare of the municipal lamps, shining on the wide pavements and on the leafless trees, emphasised the coldness of the night; and the water, lapping far below on the other side of the river wall, spoke of dismal chilliness.

But these homeless wretches were happier than Mathers, if they only knew. He was well fed and well clad in the raiment of gentility; and he had money—enough money in his pocket at that moment to translate to paradise every homeless wretch then on the Embankment. But he knew terror, whereas they knew only hunger and cold, want, misery and hopelessness.

The point at which the Bloomsbury tram-cars entered the tunnel that ran through the rising ground to the north was still a long way off. He might have boarded a car there and then, but once on the car he would feel that he was definitely on his way to Gurlitt

Row, and he was still hoping that some chance might intervene and lead him to abandon the thought of going there in favour of a better. The occupant of a condemned cell might have similar hopes.

But sometimes the impossible happens.

Mathers passed a bench that was in shadow, and in passing cast the barest glance at the bundle of humanity that sat huddled up at one end of it. One would imagine that these persons could find a place more suitable for a night's sleep than the exposed Embankment. Yet, the Embankment was the traditional home for the homeless, and Mathers supposed it would continue to be so. And because it was the traditional home, of course, they stood a chance of receiving assistance from the Good Samaritans who sometimes wandered along here with the intention of doing a few good turns. There were some amongst those high-souled individuals who came here regularly with their pockets full of half-crowns. He had heard, in fact, that the well-known psychologist, Sir Felix Quaile, would spend whole nights among the down-and-outs here with the object of making observations upon the mentality of these wrecks of humanity. Needless to say, he paid well for such knowledge as he managed to extract from them.

Mathers stopped suddenly and looked back. The shapeless bundle on the seat that he had just passed conveyed nothing to him at that distance, and he had not looked at it very closely in passing, but from some secret recesses of his mind there arose a conviction that the person on that seat was Sir Felix Quaile himself. His mind must have registered an impression that had escaped his notice at the time. Sir Felix Quaile, the renowned psychologist!

Yes, Mathers had heard that the man would even go so far as to come here actually dressed as one of the down-and-outs so far as his visible clothes went, judging thereby to be met with more sincerity.

Mathers retraced his steps, slowly, trying to avoid the appearance of too keen an interest in the man who sat huddled up on the bench. If this were indeed Sir Felix Quaile, then the man had not come here in vain on this particular night. If he wanted to study the queerer sort of psychological condition, he had chosen a fortunate time and a fortunate spot.

Mathers' heart beat quickly. Here was the chance that he had been hoping for. A man like Sir Felix Quaile was just the man who might be able to help him. Michel Benni might impose his will upon those who knew little or nothing about matters of the mind, but Sir Felix might readily be a match for him.

Yes, Mathers' heart beat quickly. And not merely from a sudden access of hope. Here was the possibility of salvation, and he wondered why he had not thought first of all about putting the case before a man who was probably competent to deal with it. But he was also moved by fear—a very definite fear. Would Michel Benni permit him to speak to Sir Felix Quaile, assuming the shapeless bundle on the bench to be the renowned psychologist?

Mathers was acutely conscious of Michel Benni's spirit. It seemed to be present in the very air. That superior will was functioning mysteriously but none the less effectively, making itself felt and filling Mathers with alarm. At any instant he expected the will to take visible form; it was quite conceivable that the image of Michel Benni might appear in front of him, preventing him from advancing another step. He might reason that the apparition was only something induced in his own mind acting under the influence of Michel Benni's mind, but that would be more than sufficient to deter him. He guessed that that might be the way in which the wizard would set to work.

The pavement, however, was still deserted. Ten or fifteen yards off was the bench on which sat the man he wanted to see. If he were able to tell his story to Sir Felix he might reasonably hope for assistance. Sir Felix would know how to deal with persons whose power lay in the regions of the mind.

He moved forward, keeping near the river wall. Before speaking to the man he wanted to make sure that it was Sir Felix and no other. A break in the wall afforded him some kind of concealment so that he could stand and study the figure on the bench.

For a long time the figure remained still, its face almost hidden on its chest, while Mathers peered from the stone recess that gave access to a flight of steps leading down to the water.

Then he stepped forward quickly. The man had altered his position, thus bringing his features into the light of one of the street lamps, and the features were unmistakably those of Sir Felix Quaile, perhaps the one man in London who could deal with Michel Benni.

CHAPTER XV

SIR FELIX QUAILE

IT WAS ONLY WHEN he had introduced himself and had been requested to sit down that Mathers could permit himself feelings of genuine relief.

It seemed that Michel Benni's power was not so very strong, after all, Mathers reflected. If he were the omnipotent person he had suggested himself to be, he would not permit this interview. He had stated that he did not mind telling his history to a handful of selected listeners because these listeners would be put under a prohibition and would find themselves unable to repeat what they had heard.

And here was Mathers already plunged into a recital of the fantastic affair and being eagerly followed by the one man Michel Benni might fear.

Once he had introduced himself, Mathers did not pay too much attention to ceremony. He did not waste time in begging Sir Felix to grant this interview; he started right away to give the salient facts—hastily, eagerly, lest Michel Benni should suddenly bring his tremendous will into play and strike the taleteller voiceless.

"Michel Benni?" Sir Felix exclaimed, sitting up straight at the first mention of the name.

"You have already heard of him, Sir Felix?" Mathers asked.

"Heard of him! But it can't be. And yet—"

"He says he has lived for over four hundred years," Mathers stated. "He discovered the secret of checking the effects of age, he says."

"That's right! That's right!" Sir Felix put in. "Michel Benni . . . We know the name well enough. And we know the history of the man. At least, we know a little of it. His activities have been observed at various times during the past four hundred years. There certainly is—or was—such a man. His last recorded appearance took place at the beginning of the past century. He was then in France. Then nothing was heard of him—until now. Michel Benni . . ."

Mathers need have had no fear about his ability to arouse the interest of Sir Felix Quaile. What had apparently been a slumbering bundle of humanity was now the alert scientist. The keenness of his intellect showed in every line of his face, making his indescribable dress incongruous beyond words.

But Mathers barely noticed the dress—the age-green overcoat that was too large for the sparse figure it covered voluminously, and the battered hat, to say nothing of the cracked, unpolished boots. He knew that the dress had all the dignity of professional raiment, for by its means this man was able to observe mental states that would be too shy to emerge in the scientific atmosphere of the consulting-room. What mattered was the intellect behind that keen face, and the fact that the keen intellect was being exercised on Mathers' behalf.

"This is really great news," Sir Felix exclaimed, rising from the bench. "Come with me. My car is just over the way. This is great news. And how fortunate that you happened to bring the news to me. Fortunate for both of us. Those who are scientifically interested imagine that Michel Benni passed away some time during the late century. We thought it more than likely that he had found his way to the guillotine, but apparently—Oh, yes, he can be killed! And I trust it will be my pleasure to kill him. There are one or two ways in which it can be done. Decapitation is one way. No man can live when his head has been cut off . . . And you say that he did not revive until the body had been taken to the flat in Regent Street from the place in Bloomsbury? That is interesting. Later, I shall ask you and your friends to give me every minutest shred of data that you have observed in this matter."

They had crossed the wide roadway by this time, and Sir Felix was holding open the door of a large, glittering car.

A policeman passed, eyeing the car and the apparently penniless beggar who was taking possession of it. Mathers feared that the apparent beggar would be accosted and asked to prove his right to the car, or that he would be taken off to the police station without being given the opportunity of making any statement; and thus a fatal delay might result. But the policeman only touched his helmet and murmured a "Good night, sir!" The habits of Sir Felix were obviously well known.

"And you can protect us?" Mathers asked.

"Why, surely!" Sir Felix replied, motioning his protégé to enter the car. "I think we can manage to settle Michel Benni. It will require certain rites that might seem to you to flavour of witchcraft—but we shall see; we shall see."

Sir Felix skirted the front of the car and climbed into the driving-seat.

"I'll take you to my place in the country," he said. "We shall be safe from interruption there, and the conditions will be more suitable in any case."

"He is probably at Gurlitt Row now," Mathers ventured.

"Quite so," Sir Felix commented. "But that does not matter. Distance is of no account in an affair of this sort. So long as I can get into touch with him on the mental plane, I can put him out of harm's way for the time being. It would take a long time for me to explain it all to you—and I doubt whether you would understand it when it was explained—but I think I can assure you, that you will have nothing to fear from Michel Benni in the future."

"You are positive, Sir Felix?" Mathers asked anxiously. And he added, apologetically: "The experiences of to-night have stamped themselves so deeply on my mind that I can't believe I'm to be released from this—this horror."

Sir Felix coughed.

"Well, I can't say positively that I'll meet with success," he admitted, as he set off at a smooth pace along the Embankment. "But I have every hope of it. Yes, I have every hope of it. With you as the bait, I can lure his mind into touch with my own. You see, it is a battle of minds. That is why I said that distance did not matter in the least. Incidentally, I can demonstrate that in a very simple way. You see that star?"

"Yes," said Mathers, looking in the direction indicated and seeing a pin-point of light through a break in the clouds.

"And you see that mascot on the radiator of the car?"

"Yes," said Mathers.

"Well, the mascot," Sir Felix pointed out, "is less than six feet away. The star is at least thirty million million miles away. You can centre your mind on the mascot in a bare flash of time. You can also centre your mind on the star in a bare flash of time. Thirty million million miles simply don't count . . . That, however, is by the way. I take it that you will place yourself unreservedly in my hands?"

"Yes," said Mathers, trying to put a note of eagerness into his voice.

After all, Sir Felix could not assure him positively that whatever was about to happen would happen for the best so far as he,

Mathers, was concerned. Perhaps Sir Felix was underestimating Michel Benni's power. Perhaps he was regarding Michel Benni as just an ordinary hypnotist—as one who could not stand against the most advanced of modern scientific knowledge and practice. And Michel Benni was an incalculable way ahead of all that the modern scientists knew. He had explained that. He had said that his mind had been developing for four hundred years, and that no mind could possibly reach the same stage of development in a normal life-span.

Mathers began to feel very uncomfortable.

"You must have faith in me," Sir Felix went on. "Without faith there might not be success, and I am most eager to lay this fellow by the heels. You cannot appreciate how much it will mean to me—to my position in the scientific world. I am, of course, eager to help you; but let me be sincere about it. You say you are grateful to me, but I also am grateful to you. This is a splendid chance for me to make some observations—some amazing observations, I have no doubt. I cannot tell you how much I welcome the opportunity. But you will have to be very brave—and very trustful. You must have implicit faith in me."

"Oh, I have!"

Mathers tried hard to put the utmost sincerity into that simple utterance, but he felt that it rang false.

"When we get to my house," Sir Felix informed him, "I shall have to leave you in a certain—a certain room, alone. You must be alone. I tell you this because it will be necessary for you to *know* that you are alone—to *feel* that you are alone."

"Alone?"

"That is one way of putting it—yes," Sir Felix said. "But I might as well be frank. Being alone, in this case, implies fear. You will be afraid. If you know that you are alone you will be profoundly afraid. And that condition is necessary to the success of the experiment."

"I—I hardly understand," Mathers said.

"Perhaps you don't," Sir Felix replied. "Your condition of mind is an important factor in the experiment, which is really a trap to catch this Michel Benni. I can reach Michel Benni's mind only by way of your mind. You and he, if all you tell me is true, are *en rapport.* You know what that means in this instance. Your two minds are working pretty much as one mind; he, at least, knows what you are thinking. And he will keep his mind in close touch with yours until he should decide to strike. My business will be to induce him to strike at a moment that will suit myself . . . However, I am perhaps going beyond your depth."

A long period of silence ensued while the car sped through South London and eventually reached the open country.

Mathers desired to gain more information, but at the same time wished he had not already been told so much. He tried hard to induce in his mind a condition of implicit faith in the man who sat by his side, but he could not succeed. Sir Felix was, first and foremost, a scientist, and to him the interest of an experiment might well be of greater importance than the safety of the subject of the experiment. Mathers knew that in thinking such thoughts he was only adding to his own fears, but he could not help it. He had a conviction that things were going to go wrong. And though he might reason himself into faith in this man's desire that the subject should suffer no more discomfort than was unavoidable, he could not reason himself into absolute faith in the man's ability to combat the power of Michel Benni.

He almost wished that he had stepped off the pavement in Piccadilly Circus—thrown himself deliberately under the wheels of a bus. Yes, he did in truth wish it. That would have put an end to everything. It would long since have been all over, and he would not now be awaiting an experience of which he knew only that it would be terrifying.

The car turned into a drive along which it sped for half a mile or more. Presently a dark mansion loomed ahead, but the car avoided the mansion, turning off down a side-road along which it ploughed at a greatly reduced speed.

"Everybody seems to have turned in for the night," Sir Felix murmured. "Which is perhaps as well," he added. "We can be sure that we will not be disturbed. I bought this place," he went on, "with the idea of having at least one spot on earth to which I could go when I wanted solitude. But I made the mistake of buying a place that was too big. It necessitates a host of servants, and servants destroy solitude. Actually the place is in the nature of a village. It even has its own chapel and burial ground, and labourers' cottages dotted here and there. By the way, we are going to the chapel now. I'll take you there and leave you in the vault. Then I'll rush back to the house. Nothing to be afraid of if you have strong nerves—and if you have complete faith in me. I don't know just what will happen, but the will of Michel Benni is almost sure to manifest itself. Try not to get into too great a panic. I think I can handle him. I say I *think* I can handle him."

By this time the car had nosed its way towards a building that stood sombrely in a small clearing in an area of woodland. This, as Mathers could see when the Norman windows were shown up for a moment in the headlights of the car, was the chapel.

Sir Felix had said that the activities might suggest witchcraft, and Mathers' heart beat unpleasantly when he saw the isolated position of the chapel and sensed the stillness of the bleak woods.

Presently Sir Felix, groping in the darkness, led him into the chapel. There he found a candle and lighted it. The faint glimmer barely defeated the gloom even of so small a place. Then, with the candle held aloft, Sir Felix led the way to a small door at one side of the altar, turned the massive key which was in the lock, and thrust the candle into his guests' hand.

"You'll find your own way down," he said, pushing open the door and disclosing a flight of steps that descended into hollow darkness. "I'll rush back to the house. Don't get into too much of a panic. You'll be all right—eventually."

Mathers took a firm grip upon himself, resisting the temptation to flee. He hesitated at the top of the stone steps, then he gave a little cry as the door was shut and the key squeaked in the lock. Faintly he heard the footsteps of Sir Felix retreating—retreating in haste. The suggestion of alarm that the haste implied brought to Mathers a sudden wave of fear. He shouted, he grasped the handle and shook the solid door; but by this time Sir Felix had reached his car, for there came through the night the violent sound of the engine, accelerating quickly; and with a diminuendo scream the car set off up that rough track to the main drive.

CHAPTER XVI

THE FATE OF MATHERS

WAS THIS PART of the plan, Mathers wondered, to bring him to the right state of terror? Or was it necessary that Sir Felix should get back to the house without delay in order to arrange the circumstances by which Michel Benni should be laid by the heels?

Mathers could only flounder in a sea of conjecture. He knew only that he felt cut off from all mankind and that he was in a state of terror and expectancy.

He stood for a long time staring down the dark stairway, then slowly and hesitatingly he began to descend. He found himself in a crypt, the floor of which was composed of large flagstones. The candle gave out but the weakest glow in the dank air of the place, but the glow was sufficient to show him that one of the flagstones had been raised and moved aside, disclosing a black cavity from which came the sound of moving water—not the pleasant bubbling of a stream, but the almost imperceptible breathing of water that moved sluggishly in eternal darkness.

On stone shelves round the walls of the vault a number of coffins had been placed, most of them ancient and mouldering. Such a feature as this was perhaps to be expected, but Mathers started back when the dim light fell on their significant outlines.

The candle in his hand was flickering. At first he thought a draught of air was causing the flickering, but presently he realized that it was due to the trembling of his own hand. He tried to check that trembling. He told himself that he must keep control of himself, for in such an atmosphere as this the first touch of panic might send a man mad. He must keep control of himself so that he might face whatever was coming. He had been living on the brink of panic for a long time now—a long time if intensity is the measure of experience. It seemed years since the attempt had been made on Michel Benni's life, and Mathers had known not one moment of peace since.

But he trusted Sir Felix Quaile. Or did he? He could not assert that he did. Sir Felix was only human, whereas Michel Benni was, in a sense, more than human.

He began to hear strange sounds—sinister sounds that might have an existence in fact or that might not. A sigh coming from emptiness. The creak of a board where no board was. And beyond these there was only the sluggish movement of the turgid water far below and the dank oppressiveness of the vault. And now he could hear his own heart, beating in a manner that shook his frame with measured jolts.

What if Sir Felix should not be able to hold the will of Michel Benni once it had been roused to activity? Mathers realized acutely that it was he himself who must pay the penalty of failure—should failure occur. Again he wished that he had had the courage to throw himself under a bus at Piccadilly Circus. For this was worse than death. Death was nothing. Death was the absence of everything—the absence of fear, the absence of doubt. But now fear and doubt had him in their grip. And the sinister atmosphere of the vault was pressing down upon him and gradually driving reason from his mind. The ghosts of those long-dead people whose coffins were mouldering on the wide stone shelves seemed to be gathering about him, gibbering and leering as though eager to claim him for their own.

And suddenly panic gripped him. Why should Sir Felix Quaile bring him here and put him into this place—and lock him in? Could one trust these scientists when scientific discoveries were imminent? Was not Sir Felix deliberately sacrificing him in order that something might be learnt about this Michel Benni? What was a solitary life—his own life—worth when compared with an important scientific discovery?

He looked wildly around. If only there was a way of escape he would flee. But there was no way of escape. There was only the cavity in the floor, with the sluggish water flowing far below.

Or if Sir Felix had dropped down dead in the meantime! People did drop down dead. Or if he had had an accident with his car! He had set off at a reckless speed towards the house, and the road was so rough that no car could cling to it while going at speed.

And in that case Mathers might be shut away from the sight of men for days and days. It was conceivable that no one might come near this deserted chapel for weeks on end. In his panic he knelt on the floor and peered over the rim of the cavity.

It was so deep that his gaze could not penetrate the lower darkness, although he held the candle at various angles so that its fight might shine downwards. Then he caught a glimmer of light reflected from the moving waters. Those waters seemed to be an immense distance down.

But so much the better, perhaps. If he were to throw himself into that hole . . . What would it mean? It would mean only one frightful moment, then he would be dashed unconscious against the sides of the well, and that would be the end. He almost welcomed the thought in spite of the emotions of revulsion caused by the water that moved in the darkness under the earth.

Then he heard a squeak—a vicious squeak—and saw the light of his candle reflected in the gleaming eyes of a large rat that was contemplating him from the depths.

With a cry of horror he staggered to his feet, gazing wildly about. No, he could not face the hideous blackness that was down there—turgid water and slime and the darkness that was infested by rats. What an end for a man to come to! No, he couldn't face it.

Then he became aware of a subtle change that seemed to have taken place in the vault. It was less a change of the disposition of the several features of the place than of the atmosphere—the sinister quality of the atmosphere. There seemed to be some force at work—some secret force that sought to claim his attention. This, he was sure, indicated the imminent manifestation of Michel Benni's will.

He gathered together the shreds of his intellectual resources. And there sprang up in him a strong faith in the ability and the sincerity of Sir Felix. The thought of the rats down below helped to strengthen that faith. It would be all right. He knew it would be all right. Sir Felix would guard him. Sir Felix had said that the manifestations would cause him extreme terror but that he must bring all his courage to the fore. He must keep in his mind the knowledge that Sir Felix was watching over him. He must stand his ground. He must not give way to panic.

For the first time he noticed that the coffins had metal plates on them—some of brass and some of silver—recording the names of those whose remains had been placed within. He did not know how these plates had formerly escaped his notice, for they were very prominently screwed to the exposed sides.

Then he remembered the words of Sir Felix relating to witchcraft. Here was evidence of apparent magic, and he knew that these plates had not been present formerly. For they all bore the same name—the name of Michel Benni. The name was followed by a date—nothing more—and the dates ranged from 1542, which was inscribed in the flowing Italian characters of Petrarch, to 1909, which was cut deep into brass that still showed its lustre. There were seven or eight coffins in all, and between each and its neighbour there was a span of about fifty years, which was roughly the apparent age of Michel Benni himself.

But Mathers had little time to consider this strange feature, startling though it might be; for he was already conscious of certain active influences at work in the shadowy vault. Vague forms were moving about him—vague wisps of darkness, rather, that had as yet no form. But he already felt that some sinister power was emanating from them.

"Now!" he breathed. "Now . . ." The manifestations were beginning. Here was the moment for bringing forth his courage. He must stand firm. He must stand firm. He trusted Sir Felix who was at the house performing Heaven alone knew what mysterious rites that would ensnare the will of Michel Benni. He had no doubts about the ability of Sir Felix. But he himself must maintain his courage.

The wisps of darkness began to take form, and Mathers saw the ghosts of Michel Benni. Not one ghost, but a number of ghosts! A ghost for every fifty years of his long existence!

On each dim face could be traced something of the development of the man's soul, and that development, from age to age, went from depravity to still greater depravity.

Courage! Courage! . . . It was all very well advising courage, but these forms were drifting slowly about him, encircling him, coming closer and closer. And their eyes were fixed on him malignantly, and sometimes they smiled as though taunting him, smiled as though they knew that he would presently give way.

But he would not give way. Something told him that as long as he could keep himself in hand he would be safe. They were still moving about him, but they were not coming nearer. Their expressions showed anger, and he would have sunk before that anger had it not been imperative that he should maintain his courage.

His knees felt weak. The strain upon his physical resources was terrific. He felt that he dared not move, for a movement would have brought him closer to these wraiths that were drifting just beyond what could be described as a magic circle that had for its centre the black hole in the floor.

An eternity seemed to pass. He tried to tell himself that his courage was not weakening, that fear was not gaining the ascendancy. But he knew that it was so. Fear was indeed gaining the ascendancy. Fear built upon doubt. The influence of Sir Felix could not be felt. Perhaps the man was unable after all to counteract the power of this wizard. Or perhaps the battle of wills would continue too long, and his own strength would fail in the meantime.

These pernicious thoughts had an immediate effect on the position, hanging delicately in the balance as it was. The wraiths were quick to take advantage of his fears—hungry to drive him to his doom. They had come perceptibly closer. If they could not be driven off they would presently touch him, and he could not bear the thought of their touching him. That would be death—worse than death.

The centre of the circle was the gaping hole in the floor. At the last he must be flung down into that blackness unless help should come to him. They would press closer and closer upon him and drive him to step into the very centre of the circle they made, and that last step would send him to perdition—down among the slime and the rats and the horror of eternal blackness.

The heel of one foot hung in space over the edge of the floor. And they were pressing upon him—they were pressing upon him. They were about to stretch out their ghostly hands and touch him. They were smiling, leering. He raised his arms to cover his face and shut out the sight of their malignant, triumphant faces. His faith was going. Panic was taking its place. Oh that he had thrown himself under that bus! He would have done so unhesitatingly had he conceived the possibility of a death like this—a death of sheer horror.

He made a last effort. He was deserted of men. Sir Felix had given no sign. He had nothing but his own strength upon which to rely. In another instant he would be gone. He opened his mouth to scream, for that might drive the wraiths off. But no sound came. They were upon him, smothering the scream ere it was born. He stepped back in a frantic effort to evade their clutches. For one awful moment he hung in space; then he was gone.

"Dunno as I can tell you," said the bundle of humanity, dressed in an age-green overcoat that was too large for the sparse figure it covered voluminously, a battered hat, and cracked, unpolished boots.

"But you were here, weren't you?" the police sergeant asked.

"As I told this 'ere constable, I was a-settin' on the bench there when the gentleman 'e comes along and goes past, then turns and comes back, a-lookin' at me like maybe 'e thought 'e knew me. Then 'e kind of stepped into this 'ere place, and next thing I knew 'e'd gone. Lost 'is balance, it struck me like; and down them stairs 'e went . . ."

"That's right, officer," said a gentleman who had just joined the small group in the recess at the top of the steps that led down to the water. "I was sitting in my car at the other side of the road—"

The body of Mathers lay on the stones. Two policemen knelt by it, pounding, pressing and massaging in an attempt to re-awaken life. At length they rose, slowly shaking their heads. From a distance came the clang of an ambulance bell.

"He couldn't have been in the water more than a couple of minutes before that boat picked him up," said the gentleman who had already spoken.

"Well, he's gone—I'm sorry," said one of the policemen who had been trying to restore life. "And look at his eyes."

He turned the body over on to its back.

"Seems like he was terrified," remarked his companion.

"It takes some that way," said the sergeant. "And some look as if they was smiling. They do say that you live through strange experiences when you're drowning . . . Make way, sir. Here's a stretcher."

Presently the clang of the ambulance bell faded again into the distance. The shapeless bundle of humanity was asked to accompany the policemen, and was promised a good lodging and good meals in exchange for his testimony, which would be required at the inquest. The derelict was in clover.

CHAPTER XVII

SUSIE SUSPICIOUS

A FEW MORNINGS later Eddie Landor came downstairs as spruce as soap and water and general vitality could make him. His sister, Susie, was in the breakfast-room alone, clad in a pink dressing-gown, sipping coffee and smoking a cigarette.

She smiled a greeting to her brother, almost without taking her glance from the newspaper that was propped up in front of her; but by the manner in which she licked her lips it was evident that she was pondering some comment discourteous with which to start the ball rolling.

A second glance at her brother, however, gave her pause. Eddie, in spite of his air of freshness, had not slept well. That was fairly obvious when one looked into his face. His manner, too, was preoccupied to a greater extent even than it had been for some time past—and that was saying something. She supposed that his preoccupation had something to do with that girl—Cynthia was her name—who had telephoned to him just before dinner a few evenings ago. Well, if this Cynthia girl had turned Eddie down, Susie reflected with a sister's partiality, then she couldn't be worth worrying about, for the very act of declining Eddie's proposal—if that were the trouble—proved her to be without a proper capacity for judgment.

Susie could not imagine that her brother's worried manner could have its cause in anything graver than a love problem. He was not the kind of boy to get into financial trouble, and she could think of no other cause whatsoever. She guessed, though, that he would tell her about it in due course.

"You want to rob me of the newspaper, I suppose?" she murmured. "While I step over and ring the bell for your breakfast to be brought in, you'll snatch the paper away, won't you?"

Eddie hardly seemed to hear. At least he did not respond to her mood.

"Please don't trouble to rise," he said. "And there's another newspaper on the sideboard; that will do perfectly."

In due course he sat down at the other end of the table. A covered dish was brought in along with fresh coffee. But even the covered dish failed to rouse Eddie from his state of preoccupation. And not least among the virtues of a silver dish-cover is its capacity for creating pleasurable suspense when one is hungry.

Without enthusiasm he addressed himself to breakfast, and without interest he turned over the pages of the newspaper.

Susie studied him surreptitiously, wondering whether she ought not to ask him straight out to tell her what was the matter with him. But before she could decide the point she saw him give a start.

"What is it?" she asked.

He looked up at her. There was certainly alarm in his expression, if not fear. He hesitated for a moment.

"You know Charlie Mathers?" he said. "You met him once, I think."

Yes, Susie remembered him. A dark-haired boy whom Eddie had once introduced to her at luncheon in an hotel somewhere.

"He's dead," said Eddie. "Drowned. Fell down some steps on the Embankment."

"Oh!" said Susie in a tense whisper while she stared at her brother.

"The inquest puts it down as death by misadventure."

"I saw something about that," Susie then said, turning back the pages of her newspaper. "I didn't pay particular attention to it."

"Death by misadventure," Eddie repeated.

The evidence at the inquest, according to the newspaper report of the proceedings, hinted at suicide. A man taking reasonable care could hardly fall down those steps. It was established, however, that the victim was in good financial circumstances, and no reason for suicide could be discovered. On the other hand, what was he doing there at that time of night? The answer to that was that he was drunk. Evidence to that effect was given by the one or two witnesses of the occurrence. He had certainly been walking about with an indecision that might have been caused by his being under the influence of drink, and in the circumstances the coroner's court took the humane view and found that death was due to misadventure.

"How shocking!" Susie murmured.

Eddie did not reply. Here was victim number one, and it would be foolish to comment on the coroner's finding. The true finding should be to the effect that Charles Mathers had been murdered by Michel Benni, but a coroner's court could never be induced to come to such a conclusion.

"Wasn't Charlie Mathers engaged to a girl named Cynthia?" Susie asked, frowning as she tried to recollect the scraps of conversation that had passed at that luncheon.

"Yes," said Eddie.

"Does that happen to be the Cynthia who telephoned to you the night before last?" As Susie asked this she looked more keenly at her brother. "It is," she exclaimed with sudden vehemence. "I know it is. I know by your manner."

"My dear girl!" he appeased her. "I never said it wasn't. It is the same Cynthia. But there isn't any need to become alarmed about it."

"Well, what's wrong?"

"What's wrong! There's nothing wrong. Why should there be anything wrong?"

Susie sat for a moment or two reflecting, and from time to time she cast a glance at her brother.

"I don't know," she said. "Only, the girl telephoned to you on the same night as Charlie Mathers met his death. Eddie, does that mean anything? Does it? If it does, tell me."

"But what could it mean?" he protested. "Charlie Mathers died at about midnight. Cynthia telephoned to me at about seven o'clock—five hours earlier. Had it been the other way round—"

"Did you see Charlie Mathers that evening?"

"Yes; as it happens I did see him."

"Oh, you did? Where?"

"At a place in Regent Street."

"Where you had dinner with Cynthia?"

"Oh, no. We met him at a friend's flat. A fellow called Forbes. Or Harringay. I don't quite know whose flat it was. Harold Crossland was there. That's Cynthia's brother."

"And what happened?"

"Nothing happened. Mathers was pretty well oiled. Drunk, I mean. But he seemed to have sobered up a good bit before we left."

Eddie had an intense desire to tell Susie all about the fantastic happenings at the flat in Regent Street. He had an intense desire to tell somebody—anybody—and particularly Susie. But some deep inhibition prevented him from mentioning the name of Michel Benni or from saying anything about the *essential* features of the meeting at the flat. It seemed that he might speak at will about the evening so long as he did not give away Michel Benni's secret. He felt that he must guard that at all costs.

"It doesn't sound to me as though that flat were a very nice place," Susie remarked. "The boy Mathers was drunk, you say. I hope, Eddie, you aren't getting into bad company. It wasn't a very nice place to take a girl, anyway."

"I didn't take her, as a matter of fact; she took me. We—"

"You must introduce me to her, Eddie. I don't know whether she sounds quite a suitable——"

"Oh, Cynthia's a splendid girl. You would like her immensely. Only, let me say what I was going to say. We went there to find her brother—Harold. She wanted to take him home. That's why she telephoned to me—to ask me whether I knew where he was. She—she was afraid he—he might be getting into trouble. About something that—that doesn't matter now."

"Oh, I see."

But Susie did not seem in any way satisfied.

"Did you think that anything tragic might happen?" she asked after a pause.

"No," he assured her. "Why should I have thought that?"

"I don't know. This isn't suicide, is it?"

A sudden gleam of hope shot through his mind. It might be suicide, after all. On seeing the newspaper report he had at once jumped to the conclusion that Michel Benni had executed vengeance upon the first of the five who had offended him. He had dismissed the idea of suicide. But why shouldn't it be suicide? Mathers was just the sort of fellow who would fly into a panic and, from sheer terror, go and drown himself.

Hence the sudden gleam of hope. The death of Mathers did not prove that Michel Benni was capable of carrying out his threat in some mysterious way of his own as had been inferred from his words. The death of Mathers did not prove anything except that Mathers was dead, and it was quite conceivable that terror had driven him to suicide.

But Susie had risen with a look of fear in her eyes.

"You're hiding something, Eddie," she exclaimed. "What is it? Tell me what it is. You know why Charlie Mathers died."

"I don't," he asserted, speaking so decidedly as almost to appear angry. "I don't, Susie—really."

She stood looking at him for a long time, then she resumed her seat with a certain self-consciousness, as though she were a little ashamed of her suspicions.

"Then it's a very extraordinary coincidence," she said, glancing at the newspaper again. "Did anything happen that night to make you think—"

"They were playing cards when we burst in on them, and they weren't quarrelling over the cards. I didn't hear that anybody had been ruined—"

"Why weren't those men—Cynthia's brother and the other men—"

"Harringay and Forbes."

"Yes. Why weren't they called to give evidence?"

"I don't know. Probably the police weren't able to trace Mathers' movements just previous to the—tragedy."

"Then why didn't they come forward and offer to give evidence?"

"For the same reason as I didn't. They probably knew nothing whatever about it."

"Eddie, I don't like the sound of this. And you needn't tell me that you don't know *anything*—that you don't know more than you've told me—because I'm sure you do. You're worried about something, whether it is something to do with this tragedy or not—"

Fortunately for Eddie his mother entered the room at that moment, and he was saved the immediate necessity of trying to convince Susie of his complete ignorance of the affair. But he could see that her suspicions were fully aroused, and he knew that she would come back to the attack.

He had never in his life kept any vital secret from his sister. But not until this moment had he appreciated to what extent the happiness of each depended upon the other. He had always simply accepted Susie as a jolly good sort. Now, however, he realized that all sisters might not be like Susie—that sisters like her were probably rare. And he realized that any tragedy affecting him would affect her equally. In fact, if the fantastic threat of Michel Benni were to be carried out to its final letter, it would be Susie who would suffer most, for he himself would be dead.

But of course the fantastic threat would not be carried out. Yet, Mathers was dead.

But that proved nothing. Mathers had gone into a blue funk and had committed suicide.

Still, he was dead. And Michel Benni had said they would die—one after another—and that Crossland would be hanged for the murder of himself, Eddie Landor.

He had not seen Crossland since that night. He had not seen any of them. He had telephoned to Cynthia's place and had made one or two calls there, but he could not get hold of either Cynthia or her brother.

CHAPTER XVIII

SKARR POINT

HAROLD CROSSLAND, too, had read of the death of Mathers.

Harold, obeying a natural impulse, had fled from London. He knew, as the others knew, that distance had no meaning in the calculations of Michel Benni, but human instinct bade him flee from the physical source of danger, and he had fled.

Moreover, he had prevailed upon Cynthia to accompany him. Strangely enough she had required little inducement. Since the night at Forbes' flat she had ceased to show more than the mildest interest in affairs—not only in the trivial matters that make up one's hour-by-hour existence, which could hardly be expected to interest her, but also in the major affair that affected them all.

At first Harold had been relieved to see that she was not adopting a violent attitude in favour of Michel Benni. The man's words had made it seem as though he had claimed her, body and soul, and Harold's fear had been lest she might leave everything and straightway become the wizard's disciple. But he was saved that distress, for the time being, at least, though it was to be expected that she would inevitably go the way mentioned by Michel Benni unless the man's fearful powers could be destroyed.

At present, however, Harold was pleased enough to know that his sister was perfectly willing to accept suggestions for her own safety, and here they were—he and she—staying in a small hotel or boarding-house in the village of Skarr Point, on the west coast of Devonshire.

Harold had told no one of this flight. Even the two maids at the Regent's Park house knew only that the brother and sister were not at home, and had been instructed to convey that vague information to anyone who might call or telephone. Hence it was that Eddie Landor had been unable to get hold of either Cynthia or her brother. And if Harold had deliberately planned the flight—as distinct from instinctively fleeing from danger—he might have done so with some idea of putting as great a distance as possible between himself and Eddie Landor. He could not forget that he was destined, according to Michel Benni, to be hanged for murdering Eddie, and it gave him some temporary satisfaction to know that Eddie was beyond his reach.

The morning was bright and the atmosphere was mild for the time of the year, and as Harold, with Cynthia by his side, sauntered out to the front of the hotel just after breakfast, he found it difficult to think seriously of the shadow that hung over their lives. The shadow—the devastating horror, rather—seemed to be something born of sheer fantasy; in the sane peacefulness of this bright morning the events of that night in Forbes' flat became unreal while still remembered; became like the recollection of a dream from which a sense of horror still lingered. Harold wondered whether he had not indeed dreamt all these things, for there was nothing present to give them point; even Cynthia's manner did not suggest that life was moving forward with anything but the most pleasant smoothness. She showed neither nervousness nor fear; she was perfectly placid, and seemed to be affected by the uneventfulness of life rather than by the expectation of terrible happenings.

The hotel stood in the midst of woods on the rising ground facing the sea. At the foot of the hill lay the straggling hamlet of Skarr Point, and beyond that lay the Atlantic Ocean, heaving peacefully on this mild morning. The hotel had only a few guests, and these few were old people who did not venture much out of doors. Harold and Cynthia were therefore left pretty much to their own devices, and they passed the time pleasantly enough, to all appearances, making the most of the restful atmosphere of the place.

A week had passed and life had fallen into a comfortable routine. In the mornings they would make the rather arduous descent to the village—for the hill was steep and the woodland path was uneven and slippery. The village was always delightful by reason of its sheer inactivity; nobody there was ever in a hurry; the people were not for ever dashing hither and thither in pursuit of the will-o'-the wisp of happiness, knowing perhaps that happiness is a timid bird that will not alight in the midst of much stir. Beyond the village and in the shelter of the headland that gave the place its name there was a natural harbour supplemented by a granite quay at which a few fishing-boats landed their catches and where an occasional coaster tied up; and invariably Harold Crossland and Cynthia found their way to this harbour which, by reason of its smallness and the fewness of its activities, was more interesting than the whole panoramic marvel of the London docks.

And when they had strolled along the little granite quay and had been absorbed—Harold, at least—by the spectacle of the two owners of the *Mary Gray* dismantling part of the engine of their craft, and had discussed weather prospects with the aged master of the *Phoebe,* they would saunter back through the village and climb the hill by way of the uneven and slippery path through the woods; and so they would arrive back at the hotel breathless and hungry, and Harold would become daily less certain about the affair at Forbes' flat.

This morning Cynthia was a little more animated than she had been since they left London. It seemed as though the change of scene was having a beneficial effect on her spirits, and this observation reacted upon Harold, who was himself feeling more normal in his outlook in consequence of leading a peaceful life in the midst of surroundings that inspired healthy thoughts.

They never discussed Michel Benni. For Harold's part he deliberately avoided mentioning the man, and Cynthia never gave any indication of remembering that such a person existed; and now she was comparatively bright, so that Harold was actually hoping that, after all, Michel Benni could be eluded and that they had, in fact, eluded him by this secret flight.

They made their way across the gravel towards the break in the woods that showed where the path began. Harold lit a cigarette—the first cigarette of the day. He was hoping that the aged master of the *Phoebe* would be on the quay. Not that he had anything of moment to discuss with the old man! He was merely looking forward to the exchange of a few chance phrases with one who was neither dullard nor don. He reflected that life at its simplest was a very satisfying affair; and he was already thinking seriously about adopting the simple life as his own.

"You like this place?" he asked Cynthia as they entered the woods.

She snatched at his arm to save herself from falling, and actually laughed with merriment as she clung to him wildly while slipping and slithering in an effort to regain a foothold.

"I do," she stated with conviction. "And *you* do."

The last words sounded almost like an accusation.

"Yes," he admitted.

This was the first time he had heard her laugh spontaneously since that memorable night.

"I'm so glad, Harold," she said. "I was thinking about that yesterday. I was wondering whether I could induce you to stay on here for a time—for a long time. If you don't mind my being personal I might say—"

"I know what you're going to say."

"You don't."

"Yes, I do. You're going to say that those fellows—Forbes and the others—aren't any good to me. And I admit it. And if you like we'll settle down here—rent a cottage, if one is available, and acquire a new philosophy."

"I should love that," she told him eagerly.

He glanced at her as she clung to him once more. She was laughing again as she faced a precipitous section of the path. The glow of health was in her cheeks and vitality seemed almost to be reflected in the silky sheen of her fair hair. There was little in her behaviour this morning to suggest that she was destined to play a part in the fulfilment of a madman's dream.

"You aren't taking Michel Benni into account any more?" he ventured to ask.

It was a risky question; but Harold could not resist putting it. If she could tell him that the influence of Michel Benni had waned to such an extent that she could regard life normally again, he could the more hopefully revise his own view of the affair. It might be, after all, that Michel Benni was no more than a skilled hypnotist who could control the thoughts and actions of people only while they were in his presence, and that his talk about holding the reins of life and death in his hands was only so much showman's patter.

At that moment even the man's remarkable recovery from the revolver shots could be argued away as a trick of some sort.

"I think you were right when you said he was mad," she answered. "And to think that I took him seriously! . . . But don't let us talk about that."

Yes, Harold could look at life in almost a normal manner this morning. Those morbid fears that had been with him for a week or more, clouding everything with horror, were fast dissolving under the influence of fresh air, healthy surroundings, and apparent peace.

He was thinking, in fact, of that money of Cynthia's that he and the others had invested. He wanted to tell her about that. A wave of virtue was affecting him. He wanted to put himself right with Cynthia. The money, fortunately, was invested in his own name and he could realize it without reference to the other three. He could tell her about it now, for in her present mood she might find it in her heart to forgive him.

That would depend, however, upon how much she had lost.

Had he thought about it earlier he would have looked at the financial pages of the morning's newspaper before he left the hotel. He had not even glanced at the papers. Last week the one or two highly speculative concerns in which the money was invested had shown an average quotation of about 50 per cent below par, and to sell out at that rate would mean that Cynthia's fortune would be halved. Still, Forbes, who knew about these things, had been optimistic, and had given it as his opinion that the shares would move quickly in the right direction when they did begin to move. They would soar overnight, he had said, though he did not expect the soaring process to take place for some months.

Harold did not immediately start to make his confession to Cynthia. Better to wait until they had got to the village and he had consulted a newspaper. Conceivably the confession might be a pleasant piece of business. If he could tell her that her fortune had been increased by about 25 per cent . . . It was, of course, a mad hope; but remarkable things did happen on the stock exchange. Or so he had been told.

At the village general shop he bought a paper—one of the few that still acknowledged the existence of a certain intelligence among the readers of newspapers. He opened it casually while he and Cynthia strolled towards the quay. But he did not happen to open it at the financial pages right away, and the fortunes of the concerns in which he was interested became a matter of secondary importance.

For some moments he continued to walk by Cynthia's side—to walk mechanically, quite unaware of movement. Then he paused.

"I meant to buy some cigarettes," he said. "You go on. I'll join you in a minute or two."

He was surprised at the readiness of his invention. But he had to be alone for a moment.

Mathers had been killed.

Cynthia did not notice his alarm. She continued on her way to the quay. He slowly retraced his steps to the village street, trying hard to keep a grip upon himself.

Mathers had been killed.

The news, coming unexpectedly as it did when it seemed that Michel Benni had been eluded, had a staggering effect. They said that Mathers had died through misadventure. That meant an accident. The evidence seemed to be clear enough. It was clear enough, at any rate, to impose upon the coroner, who would be a man not easily imposed upon. But Harold knew that the death was no accident.

CHAPTER XIX

TRUNK CALLS

THE GENERAL SHOP was also the post office, and had a public telephone installed. It was natural that Harold—his fears violently aroused by this warning of danger—should wish to get into touch with the others who shared the danger. He knew Forbes' number, and he did not have to spend time in making enquiries on that score; but he did have to spend a considerable time in waiting to be connected with the flat in Regent Street.

The telephone was eventually answered, but not by Forbes. Forbes had a moderately high-pitched voice, and the tones that came over the wire seemed to rumble from some hollow-sounding cavern.

"Hallo, Harringay!" Harold cried. "This is Crossland. You know about Mathers?"

There followed a pause, then the deep voice rumbled again.

"Who are you? What name did you say?"

"Crossland. You've heard about Mathers?"

"Crossland? Where are you speaking from?"

"Never mind about that, Harringay. Is Forbes there?"

"Well, in a sense—yes."

"In a sense?"

"My name isn't Harringay, though. Do you happen to be a friend of Mr. Forbes?"

"Yes. What's the matter? Who are you?"

Harold was puzzled—no more than that at first. But in a flash he guessed that something was amiss.

"Who are you?" he repeated, and the staccato words were a cry of alarm.

There was no direct reply, but he could hear whispering or hurried conversation being carried on close to an inadequately-covered mouthpiece.

"We're the police," the rumbling voice then said with sudden loudness. "You are a Mr. Crossland, I understand?"

"Yes."

"Would you care to give me your address, Mr. Crossland? We want to get into touch with as many of Mr. Forbes' friends as possible."

Harold gave his address, adding that he was at present on holiday in Devonshire. He gave those particulars almost subconsciously while eagerly impatient to know what was the matter.

"Well, I'm sorry to have to tell you, Mr. Crossland," the voice went on, "that Mr. Forbes is dead. He's been found shot. In his flat, here. A revolver was in his hand . . . Did I hear you mention the name of Harringay, Mr. Crossland?"

"Yes," said Harold, paying barely any attention to the last question. Even the physical properties of the things immediately about him—the telephone box with its glass panels, the haberdashery on the shelves of the shop, the little section of counter devoted to postal business—these hardly impressed themselves on his consciousness. Forbes had committed suicide. Forbes and Mathers were dead—in accordance with Michel Benni's prediction. That left Harringay. And Eddie Landor. And himself. And it was said that he would be hanged for the murder of Eddie. "Did he commit suicide?" he asked.

"That I can't say, sir," the policeman answered. "He was found shot through the head, and he had a revolver in his hand—the revolver that killed him, by the look of it. But I won't say it was suicide."

"Then was it murder?"

"I can't say that either."

"You mean you aren't sure?"

"No. I simply mean, sir, that it isn't for me to play the part of coroner."

"I see. But suicide is indicated. If you were free to state your own opinion you would say it was suicide—"

Harold did not know why he should trouble to speak like that. What the police officer thought was of no consequence. But that Harold did seriously bend his mind to the unimportant question of whether the death could be put down to suicide showed that, for the moment, his own mental processes were evincing themselves without his reasoned control.

"I hardly think so, sir," said the officer. "Sometimes murder is made to look like suicide. You mentioned a Mr. Harringay, I think."

"But you don't mean to say—"

"It isn't my place to give verdicts."

"Harringay didn't murder Forbes."

"We had no intention of connecting Harringay with Forbes, but now that you mention the name, sir—"

"Harringay didn't murder Forbes," Harold repeated.

"It isn't that," said the officer. "As I say, we had no intention of connecting Harringay with Forbes. But now that you say they knew one another—if the Harringay you're thinking of is the same as the Harringay I'm thinking of—it puts a new complexion on the affair. A man of the name of Harringay was run over by a bus just outside here not an hour ago. He was killed instantly. Would you care to describe the Harringay you have in mind, sir . . ."

Harold did describe him. He described him in a few words, but with no doubts regarding the identity of the man who had been run over by a bus and killed.

Some time later he left the post office and wandered off towards the quay in search of Cynthia. His fears had returned tenfold. Michel Benni was carrying out vengeance without delay—Mathers a week ago, and now Forbes and Harringay! He was not aware of exertion as he walked towards the place where he knew he would find Cynthia. His senses were numbed by horror.

But his brain was clear enough, and he was thinking furiously. He had not given the police his present address, and while he stayed here he would not be able to kill Eddie. That was one fact that stood out plainly. The police wanted to interview him, though, and they might insist upon his going to London. He had promised to report to the local police station, and he supposed he had better do that though he knew that he dared not tell the truth. Michel Benni's power still held good. He felt it. He felt it in his reluctance to go there and then to the police and tell them exactly what had happened. He knew that he would not be able to speak the words that would bring Michel Benni into the affair. And though he were to do so he would not be believed. The police would hardly base a conviction upon the statement that a man who had lived for over four hundred years was sending other men to their death simply by the exercise of willpower.

But he must tell the police something. They would know by his manner that he knew something. Very well! He would say that they had all been swindling Cynthia and were in immediate fear of being found out, and had apparently committed suicide as the only way out of their difficulties.

The aptness of that story—which he could prove by his recorded dealings in shares—startled him, frightened him. It was just such an explanation of the deaths as would be ready at hand to safeguard the secret of Michel Benni.

Yet, might not these men—Mathers, Forbes and Harringay—have actually committed suicide from fear? It was possible. It was indeed probable. He recalled the substance of Michel Benni's remarks on that memorable night. The man had said that he would find diversion in exercising his ingenuity in devising the several means of death. But to Harold's way of thinking the deaths had all been very ordinary in their circumstances. There had been nothing about any of them to warrant much preliminary thought on the part of a man who possessed a brain that had been developing for four centuries. Mathers had thrown himself into the river; Forbes had shot himself with a revolver; and Harringay had thrown himself under a bus. Surely a man with absolute power, wishing to amuse himself, could conceive deaths much more spectacular and terrible than these!

But Harold had no knowledge of the agelong seconds just preceding death, when whole chapters of horror could be lived through.

Cynthia was not on the quay. Old Jim, the master of the *Phoebe,* said she had gone back to the village by way of the foreshore. Harold stood for a few minutes in conversation with Old Jim, then he saw Cynthia approaching.

She did not show curiosity respecting the length of time he had taken to buy cigarettes. She said no more than that they had better be getting back to the hotel.

She did not seem to notice that there was anything amiss. He felt that no one could fail to see how violently troubled he was, but Cynthia did not see it. For that he was glad. Cynthia was existing under the happy impression that they had succeeded in breaking away from the strange influence of Michel Benni, and he would take all possible steps to conceal from her the knowledge of the three deaths that had already taken place.

And conceivably they had succeeded in breaking away from the influence of Michel Benni. The three deaths, by their very ordinariness, seemed to point to suicide on the part of the three men rather than murder on the part of Michel Benni.

He opened the newspaper again, solely in order to avoid the necessity of making conversation. He turned to the financial pages, remembering that it was for the sake of the financial pages that he had bought the paper. And in spite of his abnormal emotional state he got a thrill from what he saw there. The tide had turned, as

Forbes had said it would. But much earlier than Forbes, at his most optimistic, had thought possible. A sudden demand for the commodity in which the money was invested had put the shares many points above par, and where between twenty and thirty thousand pounds were involved the gain was considerable.

Still keeping in touch with the practical affairs of existence, he decided to telephone to his brokers immediately he returned to the hotel and instruct them to sell out.

And if this could be taken as an augury, he could look upon life with more confidence. In fact, it had already started to encourage confidence. He would make his statement to the police during the afternoon. They would probably ask him to attend the inquests, and after that he would continue to keep himself at a safe distance from Eddie Landor. And he would keep Cynthia by his side.

His plans for the future were in a measure hopeful, although they were not definite. He was trusting to the gradual waning of Michel Benni's power. He knew that hypnotic influence waned unless it were kept alive by periodical exercise, and in the case of himself and Cynthia that power had not been apparent during a whole week, and that perhaps argued that they had evaded Michel Benni by this secret flight.

Yes, Harold was certainly inclined to be hopeful. He did not know that flight from Michel Benni was impossible. Nor did he know that Cynthia, while he was making his way towards the quay, was in the post office telephoning to Eddie Landor, moved by an intense desire to tell Eddie where she was and thrilled when he said he would come down to Devonshire by the very first train, bringing his sister with him.

CHAPTER XX

THE THIRD TRAVELLER

IT WAS SUSIE LANDOR who was puzzled by the trend of events that evening. The others—her brother Eddie, and Harold and Cynthia Crossland—were not puzzled. They were too deeply involved for that. They knew what was afoot, for the events had been forecast plainly enough. And they knew, individually, that none of them could alter these events or flee from them or evade their consequences.

The guest-house—it was more in the nature of a guest-house than an hotel—had been a middle-class residence at one time in its history, and it had been but slightly altered to conform with modern ideas of comfort. Half a dozen bathrooms had been installed, making a total of seven; the four-poster beds had been sold to dealers in curios; and the candelabra had been modified towards the end of the late century so that the more serviceable oil lamps could be brought into use. But the owners of the place did not consider that further modernization was necessary or even desirable. Devonshire was Devonshire, after all; and a house in the woods, close to a little fishing village of thatched cottages, would lose a great deal of its charm if it were fitted with a cocktail bar and lighted by electricity.

Not that cocktails could not be had! But he who felt the need for them was looked at sideways by the permanent guests, who were all elderly and who had formed settled habits before cocktails were invented.

Susie Landor, however, was not aware of the aversions of the permanent guests; and though she rarely took either stimulants or appetizers, being normally intelligent, she knew that there were times when nerves could best be brought under control by artificial means, and she was ready to suggest that the ritual of dining might be preceded by the ritual of cocktail drinking on this occasion.

What was wrong with the others she could not make out. But she was sure that something was wrong. Four young people thrown together like this would normally have few restraints.

Modern life was such as to create intimacy at short notice or no notice at all among those of the same class. But here there was a definite restraint as though the other three held a secret that she was not permitted to share.

It had started with Eddie himself while they were still at Waterloo station. He had been looking forward with the liveliest enthusiasm to this journey to Devonshire, and the haste with which it had been arranged helped to make his enthusiasm more noticeable. It appeared that the girl—Cynthia Crossland—had gone away without letting him know where she was going, and her unexpected telephone call had released the tension and had thrown him into the highest spirits.

But something had occurred at the station.

They were looking for an empty compartment, but as it happened there was not one even in the first-class sections of the train. Every one seemed to have at least two persons in it, and the British travelling public seeks to avoid company rather than to welcome it. Susie, however, did discover a compartment containing only one traveller—an elderly man with a beard of the imperial type, who looked like a foreigner and who might not know enough English to be a bore.

But as he was about to open the door, Eddie paused. She saw him glance once at the foreign-looking gentleman and she saw him start. Whether a look of recognition passed between the two she could not tell. The man seated in the compartment seemed to smile vaguely, but gave no other positive sign of acknowledgment. Eddie, on the other hand, withdrew from the neighbourhood of the compartment with no attempt at doing so gracefully. He put forward no explanation but simply retreated from the compartment and presently found two corner seats in another.

Susie might not have thought a great deal about the incident had it ended there. One did sometimes form unreasonable aversions towards strangers, and the present could possibly be an instance of that. But she thought it curious if not significant that from that moment Eddie's high spirits vanished. During the journey down he spoke listlessly when he spoke at all, but for the greater part of the time he read, or pretended to read, the magazines and books they had brought with them.

Darkness had fallen by the time they reached their destination. Outside the little station a large, old-fashioned car was waiting for them, having been sent by the hotel. But the car was not for them alone, Susie discovered. It was for the general use of guests arriving. And in this case it had one passenger besides themselves—the elderly, foreign-looking man whom they had seen at Waterloo.

This fact struck Susie as being very singular in the light of Eddie's behaviour at the London terminus. Beyond that there was nothing remarkable in the man's appearing now, for the train was the most convenient one of the day as it happened and would naturally be selected by an intending visitor to the hotel.

The short run in the car was completed almost in silence by the little party of guests. The elderly man spoke not at all except to murmur a gracious word when they were about to alight and he forestalled Eddie in opening the door.

They met the Crossland brother and sister in the entrance hall.

Susie could not but regard critically the girl whom Eddie was so interested in, but her opinion of Eddie as a man of sound judgment was maintained. Cynthia Crossland, advancing through an open doorway, along with her brother, to greet the visitors, had all the charm of sincerity without which mere prettiness is quite ephemeral in its effect. Yes, Eddie was obviously a man of sound judgment, even in the matter of selecting his girl friends—a matter in which judgment is so apt to go awry.

For a moment or two the little party of four stood in a group in the hall. Cynthia and her brother were talking animatedly, and in the excitement of the introductions Susie quite forgot the third passenger in the car, who had remained behind in conversation with the chauffeur. But now the door opened and he came in.

With his arrival a hush fell on the group. It was as though they were a group of chattering servants surprised by the master of the house. Susie had been about to say something, but the sudden hush made her pause as one would if a warning of danger had been whispered. The new arrival stepped past the group then vanished, under the directions of the hall porter.

But chatter did not recommence. Eddie put in a word or two, but his remarks were not taken up by the others. Harold Crossland suggested that they should see about their rooms, and the party moved off.

Susie wondered. It did not seem to coincide with reason, but it did appear to her that their fellow-guest had cast a pall over the group. She could not understand it, but she had to accept her own observations. As far as she could see, the foreign-looking guest was quite a normal person. His eyes had a kind of glitter in them, perhaps; but this was not unusual in a native of one of the Latin countries, as this man probably was. He had said nothing that could cause him to be regarded as anything but an ordinary man; he had, in fact, taken no notice of the group. Yet, undoubtedly, he had had a profound effect upon them.

Susie might have paid less attention to this had she not already observed a similar phenomenon in the case of Eddie at Waterloo station. First it had been Eddie, and now Cynthia and Harold Crossland. It was very strange.

She and Eddie went into the little office in order to go through with the registration of their names in the books of the place. She had Eddie to herself for a few moments.

"Who is that man?" she asked bluntly.

"Man?" Eddie echoed.

"That man who came up with us in the car—the man we saw at Waterloo—"

"I don't know," said Eddie with a forced laugh. "How should I know?"

"Why did you avoid him at Waterloo?"

"Didn't care for the look of him perhaps."

"I thought he smiled when you opened the compartment door then turned away."

"I didn't notice it," Eddie stated. "If he did it was probably because he thought we were a honeymoon couple. Honeymoon couples invariably cause other people to smile."

"You aren't telling me the truth, Eddie," she murmured, looking at him keenly.

He shrugged his shoulders, and his expression said that he was at a loss to know why Susie should speak like that, but if she cared to think that he was not telling the truth then he could do nothing to convince her otherwise.

But in his heart his feelings were vastly different. He would have given all he had in the world to be able to tell Susie that the man to whom she referred was Michel Benni and that he had come down here to claim Cynthia; that by what was apparently a perfectly natural series of events Cynthia and Harold and he, Eddie, had been brought together in this out-of-the-way place in order that the prediction of Michel Benni might be conveniently fulfilled. He longed to tell Susie of the curse that lay over them, and to warn her that he was about to be killed by Harold Crossland, who would be hanged for the murder, and to tell her that Cynthia was destined to become the helpmate of Michel Benni and the mother of a race of monsters who would drive all sanity from the face of the earth. But a will more powerful than his own kept his tongue in check, and against his reason he had to strive to keep his secret and, by any subterfuge, impress Susie with the conviction that everything was as normal as it could be.

"Why on earth should I be telling anything but the truth?" he exclaimed.

"I don't know," she said. "I don't know why you should be telling me anything but the truth. I only know that you are. You're hiding something. You're pretending that you don't know that man, but you do. And the Crosslands know him as well. Who is he? Why is he here? Why did you all stop talking when he came in?"

Eddie looked disarmingly perplexed.

"Really, Susie, I haven't the faintest notion of what you're driving at."

But Susie, signing the register, found the answer to at least one of her questions. The man's name was Michel Benni. There it was, written just above her own in a bold, angular hand, that reminded her of the signatures one sees on historical documents in museums. The name, however, conveyed nothing to her; and as Eddie persisted in maintaining that he knew naught of the man, she had to assume that her suspicions were false.

But she knew that they were not false.

CHAPTER XXI

The Cocktail

WHEN THE COMPANY of four young people met in the lounge just before the hour of dinner the same mysterious restraint was upon three of them.

The lounge was quiet, although most of the guests had gathered there preparatory to being summoned to the dining-room. Those who spoke spoke in whispers, possibly so that they might not drown the announcement of dinner, and the hush created an atmosphere suggesting the imminence of startling events.

"They don't have dancing here," said Harold Crossland, speaking chiefly to Susie Landor. "They dine, then they set aside an hour for digestion's sake, then they go to bed."

"That's just like mother," Susie commented, turning to her brother.

"A home from home," said Eddie.

"What shall we do to-morrow?" Cynthia asked, perhaps conscious of the absence of verve in the atmosphere and wishing to put some enthusiasm into life for the sake of the new visitors. But Susie could tell that half of her mind was elsewhere.

"To-morrow never comes," said Harold, with apparent pointlessness.

He did not himself know why he should make such an utterly banal remark. But, banal or not, it had a tremendous effect on Eddie.

They were standing in a group close to one of the walls. Eddie was half leaning against a piano whose lid was fully open. He had been glancing with mild interest at the strings that were thus disclosed, but suddenly he stood up straight.

"Was that remark necessary?" he asked, and he looked at Harold in a way that might almost suggest annoyance.

Susie looked puzzled for a moment, as though she thought her brother's look of annoyance might be assumed for the purpose of some ponderous joke or other, albeit she knew that ponderous jokes were inexcusable among cultured people.

But she saw that Harold Crossland was very serious.

"Not exactly necessary, perhaps," he said. "But true, nevertheless. To-morrow never does come, does it? To-morrow becomes to-day whenever it arrives."

Eddie shrugged his shoulders and went so far as to give something like a snort as though to indicate contempt for such childish talk.

"Oh, the words can be applied in other senses," Harold was quick to point out, and there was something almost pugnacious in his manner. Susie was amazed.

"That is to say?" Eddie prompted.

He spoke the words in a manner that hinted at lofty patronage towards the man who was supposed to be his friend.

"That is to say," Harold Crossland took him up, "that for some people—many people—to-morrow will never dawn at all, call it tomorrow or to-day or what you like."

"I see," said Eddie. "I'm being warned, am I?"

"Eddie!" Susie exclaimed. "What on earth's the matter with you?"

She regretted intensely having to acknowledge openly that a quarrel of some sort existed, but she was so amazed that she could not help it. She was amazed, too, by the attitude of Cynthia Crossland. Cynthia was regarding the two men as though nothing out of the ordinary were happening. She seemed to exist in a world of her own where men seething on the brink of a violent quarrel were simply not comprehended.

"Have they all been taking drugs?" Susie asked herself.

"I'm so sorry, Miss Landor," Harold Crossland made haste to say.

But he did not put forward any explanation of the strange scene. He merely turned back his cuff and looked at his wristwatch and compared it with the ornate clock that stood on the mantelpiece.

"I think Eddie wants a cocktail," Susie remarked. "But I suppose such things are blissfully unknown here."

"What a splendid suggestion!" Harold exclaimed, taking a step towards the door. "I wonder whether such things are available." Then he paused and glanced at his companions interrogatively. "What particular blends are required?" he asked.

Cynthia and Susie each mentioned one of the milder varieties. Eddie hesitated.

"What about a Corpse Reviver?" Harold suggested.

After a further hesitation Eddie nodded.

"Be it so," he said. "And there is a splendid tip for you," he added.

"For me?" Harold asked.

"Yes. Bear it in mind. When the warder comes in and asks what you'll have for breakfast—tells you that on this unique morning you can have whatever you want—"

Harold ignored the taunt, turned on his heel and went out of the room.

"Whatever's the matter with you, Eddie?" Susie demanded.

Eddie shrugged his shoulders.

"Nothing," he said.

"Is all this serious? Or are you two playing some game? I confess I'm utterly at a loss."

"It is quite all right, my dear," Eddie replied with a smile.

But the smile was not a genuine expression of his feelings. The eyes behind the smile held what was probably a genuine expression of his feelings, and they seemed to show a soul sunk deep in trouble.

"Quite all right?" she echoed. "Mr. Crossland seems to be hinting at killing you before to-morrow, and you say that it is quite all right."

"That isn't what he's hinting at," Eddie assured her.

But he failed to give any other explanation of the strange words that had passed, and Susie wondered whether her former suspicion about drugs was not the true one. In any case, looking squarely at the matter, she could hardly imagine that Harold Crossland was threatening to kill Eddie. They were supposed to be very good friends; but even assuming that the friendship had split on the rocks, it was surely not such a serious matter as might, in their view, justify the murder of one or the other. Or, if it were, they surely had more sense than to speak about it openly. Yes, openly. The threats and remarks were so thinly veiled as to be fully exposed in all their stark meaning. They could not possibly be serious in these threats.

Susie received no light from Cynthia. Cynthia had not been listening to what was passing between Eddie and his sister. Her attention was on the door; and Susie, looking in the same direction, saw the elderly Michel Benni enter.

The man sauntered some way into the room, then sat down in a vacant easy-chair. He took no notice of anybody.

And presently Harold Crossland returned, carrying a tray on which were four glasses.

"The rule here is that drinks are not brought to you by the staff, except at table," he explained. "The bulk of the establishment's clientele is extremely respectable and easily offended as to its moral code. So the establishment makes rules that flatter these excellent people's prejudices. If you want a cocktail you've to go and fetch it. The establishment can't refuse to supply drinks, but it supplies them, as it were, under protest. You must, as I say, go and fetch them—and brand yourself decadent. The fault is with you—not with the management."

He offered the tray to the girls, who each took a glass. Susie was aware that all the other people in the room were regarding the tray with looks of disapproval—all except the elderly man who had come down from London that day. He was quietly studying the fire, round which a group was gathered.

"Not only that," Harold Crossland went on, offering the tray to Eddie, who took the Corpse Reviver, "but if you want cocktails you have to mix them yourself."

Cynthia gave a slight start. A look of fear came into her eyes for a second as she turned and glanced at Eddie, who was holding his glass up to the light and studying it critically. She raised one hand a little way with a quick movement as though she would touch Eddie's arm, then she relapsed into her former attitude of listlessness.

Harold continued to talk. It was as well, he said, that he was experienced in the art of cocktail mixing. Yes, he had to admit that he was experienced. It was an art that could be cultivated only at a great expense, he didn't mind saying. Still, the knowledge of compounding drinks came in useful at times.

It seemed to Susie that Harold Crossland was trying to make up for the general strangeness of the party by talking at length upon the first subject he could think of.

Presently the gong went. The shade of a sigh heaved through the lounge and people began to stir. Susie sipped the last inspiring drops of the concoction mixed by Harold, and complimented Harold on his skill.

He bowed his acknowledgments.

"But Eddie doesn't think much of it," he said.

"Why, he hasn't even tasted his," Susie exclaimed.

Eddie did not answer. He strode towards the fireplace, whence the other guests had departed, and with a leisurely flick of his wrist threw the contents of his glass into the red-hot coals. The liquor sizzled for a moment, sending up a little cloud of steam and dust. Then he strode back and placed the empty glass on the tray. In doing so he looked long and steadily at Harold.

Then they all retired to the dining-room.

CHAPTER XXII

Room 11

BY TEN O'CLOCK all the regular guests had gone to bed. Of the four young people, Susie Landor felt very tired after her day of travelling, and had the circumstances been the normal circumstances attending a holiday she too would probably have retired soon after dinner.

But the circumstances were anything but normal, and she was afraid to retire. That was the truth, as she had to admit—she was afraid to retire.

During the dinner the feud, or whatever it was that existed between her brother and Harold Crossland, had lain dormant. The two men exerted themselves to make the meal a success, and it would have been quite a pleasant affair so far as Susie was concerned had it not been for the preposterous shadow that hung over the little party. Susie did not use the epithet loosely. The shadow really could be described, according to her observations, as preposterous. There was something of the absurd in the whole business. Her own original suspicions had been based on the incident at Waterloo—an incident that was absurdly slight. The remarks exchanged between her brother and Harold Crossland had been quite absurdly pointed, for either they meant nothing or they meant everything, and if they meant everything they would never have been uttered by men in their senses. It was further absurd that the appearance of that man, Michel Benni, should affect these three as it had done, for the man had said nothing to them and had taken no notice of them. And perhaps the most absurd thing of all was that the whole party seemed now to be on the best of terms.

In the midst of such a preposterous set of circumstances Susie did not know what to do. She knew only that she could not go to her room and go to bed and sleep. She must first of all satisfy herself that Harold Crossland's threats had not been made seriously.

Immediately they rose from dinner she slipped into the lounge. The significance of Eddie's act in throwing his cocktail into the fire had just occurred to her. It was so fantastic that she had not thought of it until this moment. She had assumed the act to be a gesture—a very churlish gesture—on the part of Eddie to show how he despised Harold's hospitality. But it was not that. It was that he thought the drink to be poisoned.

So she slipped into the lounge with the object of obtaining the glass that had held the drink. There would still be some drops clinging to the sides of the glass, and these could be analysed. They could not be analysed that night, but the next day it would still be possible to know whether the drink had been poisoned, even though the drops of liquid had dried.

As she entered the lounge she felt that her face had gone white. To think that anybody would poison a drink intended for Eddie! Eddie, she was sure, would never do anybody an injury. The fellow Crossland must be mad. Perhaps that was the explanation. Assuming the drink to be poisoned and assuming Eddie to have drunk it and to have died in consequence, Harold Crossland could not fail to be convicted of murder. He said he had mixed the drinks himself, and that damning fact could easily be verified.

But the tray of glasses had gone.

They were probably washed up by this time, but in any case Susie could not create alarm by going through to the kitchen quarter to enquire. And there was no need to. In the midst of this fantastic affair there was one act that she could judge at its proper value and that was Eddie's act of throwing the cocktail into the fire. Nothing would have made him do that ungracious act except the knowledge that the drink had been poisoned or the knowledge of the reasonable probability of its having been poisoned. Which meant that he *knew* that Harold Crossland was trying to kill him.

The utter absurdity of the whole affair notwithstanding, that fact had to be admitted.

She rejoined the other three in the hall, where the two men were amusing Cynthia with the kind of light talk that had been carried on throughout dinner. They were all behaving now in quite a normal manner.

"Who says a hand at cards?" Harold asked.

"That's a good idea," Susie agreed. "Is there a card-room?"

"No," Harold told her. "We make do in the lounge. There's a billiards-room and there's a writing-room. The writing-room and the lounge are the nearest the management will go towards making the place like a hotel."

"I see," said Susie. "So they would be shocked beyond measure if we were to make it an all-night sitting—"

"Oh, shocked beyond measure!"

"A pity. I feel perfectly fresh. And I think an occasional all-night sitting does one good. Don't you?"

"Well—"

"There's something salutary in breaking away from routine," Susie continued. "Even good habits are the better for being disturbed now and again. Habits take possession of one and are rather apt to dull the senses."

"My dearly beloved sister," said Eddie, "the Devonshire air has assuredly played havoc with your normally sound philosophy."

"My dear, inconsistent brother," she replied, "for years you have been trying to invent acceptable reasons for staying out late at night, and when I give you one that mother might swallow you say I'm talking rubbish."

Eddie looked at her with mock grimness.

"As we are in a semi-public place," he said, "I suppose I mustn't pinch you or throw cushions at you or otherwise express myself suitably. Let me say simply that the day's travelling has made me quite ready for bed, and that I don't care how soon I get there."

"In that case—" Cynthia Crossland began.

"But being a gentleman," Eddie interrupted, "I conceal my real desires and say that nothing will give me greater pleasure than to sit up for an hour or two making the necessary fourth. So shuffle the cards, Harold."

The party, with every appearance of innocent jollity, moved towards a small table. Then Harold had to look for a pack of cards.

While he was doing this Susie excused herself on the pretext of going to her room for a handkerchief. She hastened out of the lounge and went straight to the office, almost colliding with their fellow-guest, Michel Benni, who was then sauntering through the hall. The man inclined his head courteously and passed on. Susie wondered whether she were right in imagining that this quiet, unobtrusive person had in fact caused the reactions that she thought she had observed in the others. His manner, as far as she was concerned, was quite ordinary, and either he had nothing to do with the strange atmosphere and the strange behaviour of the others or he had much to do with it, and in the latter case he was a man of profound depth—a man whose very calmness was rather fearful to think about.

She passed on towards the office.

Why hadn't Eddie fallen in with her suggestion for an all-night sitting? She knew that the arguments she had put forward were the sheerest nonsense, but if he had pretended to agree with them the others would have been forced to do the same. Hadn't he seen that she was trying to protect him? Did he or did he not believe that Harold Crossland intended to kill him? Did he want to be killed? Was there any sanity in the whole perplexing affair?

Whatever it was all about, she must do everything in her power to prevent a tragedy. She would have called in the police, but what could she say to the police? She could only mention her suspicions, and in the cold light of reason these suspicions became very flimsy. The police would laugh at her fears, telling her that a prospective murderer does not advertise his intentions in public and that the whole thing must be a joke on the part of the two men. Moreover, she had a conviction that Eddie would not support her story if the police were called in. Nor would Cynthia Crossland. Cynthia's reactions were so placid that the slightly-veiled threats of murder seemed to have disturbed her not at all.

But something had to be done.

The office was in the charge of a middle-aged man of austere bearing who might easily be a local churchwarden. Susie did not regard him very hopefully as being a man likely to agree with the suggestion she had to make. If he had been a young man he might have been susceptible to blandishments; she could usually induce young men to grant such favours as she might ask. But a churchwarden was a different matter.

"My brother has room 15, I think," she said when the churchwarden gave her an enquiring look and a wintry smile. "Mr. Landor is the name."

"Ah, yes!" said the churchwarden, referring to a large book.

"I wonder whether you could put him somewhere else?" Susie asked.

The churchwarden glanced at her in surprise.

"As to that, madam," he said, "we must see. Does Mr. Landor consider room 15 unsuitable?"

"Oh, we aren't complaining," Susie hastened to say. "It looks a very comfortable room. But it is rather exposed—on a corner of the building. And my brother is rather delicate. Perhaps you have another you could let him have. The one next to mine, for instance."

The churchwarden referred to his book again.

"You are in number 10, madam. The room you mean is number 11. Unfortunately it is occupied already, but—"

"Oh, in that case—"

The churchwarden glanced at the girl out of the corner of his eye. A secret smile played about his mouth.

"Oh, no, it isn't!" he said. "I made a mistake. Yes, Mr. Landor may certainly have number 11."

"That's awfully good of you," Susie was quick to say, clinching the favour before it should be withdrawn. "There's just one thing," she went on. "Don't tell him that I asked you to do this. He might not like it. He's rather—rather cantankerous, if I may say so in confidence. He might resent my interference. Please just tell him that a mistake has been made and that his things have been transferred to room 11. You can tell him that when he comes in for his key. I hope I'm not putting you to too much trouble."

"It isn't any trouble at all," said the man, looking at Susie narrowly. "But Mr. Landor won't have to come in here for his key. The keys are all in the doors of the rooms. It isn't as if this were a hotel, you see, madam."

"Oh—I understand. But I'll send him in all the same. He doesn't know but what the keys are kept here. Then you can tell him about the change of room."

"Very good, madam."

Leaving the office, Susie hastened up the stairs.

She had succeeded in having Eddie's room changed, and that was a point of some importance. If the change could be kept from Harold Crossland, Eddie would probably be safe for one night at least. If Harold Crossland contemplated coming forth when the place was asleep, silently entering room number 15, and there overpowering Eddie, he would find himself drawn up short. Eddie would not be there, and Harold Crossland would hardly make a stealthy search of all the rooms. The risk in doing that would be too great.

There was, however, the chance that Harold Crossland would see Eddie going into room 11. Susie was already planning to hold Harold Crossland in conversation downstairs while Eddie went off to bed, so that the change in the rooms might not be known; but she might not be able to carry that part of the business through successfully, so she had thought of a supplementary plan that would positively ensure Eddie's safety.

She could ask him to lock his door on the inside. But in his present strange state he might refuse to lock his door. So to make sure that it was locked she would lock his door.

She was now going upstairs to possess herself of the key, thinking it a piece of very good fortune that the place was run more as a private house than as a hotel. And when Eddie should have retired for the night she would lock the door on the outside and retain the key. Then Harold Crossland could do his worst.

She had no difficulty in removing the key from the door of room 11, for there was no one about when she ascended the stairs; the soft rays of an oil lamp affixed to the end wall illuminated a silent and deserted corridor.

Presently she rejoined the group in the lounge.

As she entered, there seemed to be a general move by the other guests towards turning in for the night. The time was getting on for ten o'clock. By the time the card party was settled the lounge was empty save for the four card-players and one other—Michel Benni, who was reclining deep in an easy-chair in front of the fire and who seemed to be entirely occupied with his own thoughts.

Meanwhile, the austere person in charge of the office was reflecting upon the deplorable state of youth these days. In the capacity of resident manager of this select home-from-home he frequently had occasion to criticize youth and the modern world generally. He knew that people's morals were appalling and that even the utmost vigilance on the part of one such as he could not protect these morals. But he did his best. He refused in a downright manner to be a party to any questionable conduct that might be contemplated under his roof, and where his suspicions were verified he sent the culprits forth.

But people were so clever in wrongdoing that it was not always possible to circumvent or even detect them. Their trickery was infinite. But he knew many of their dodges. Sometimes they represented themselves as husband and wife. And sometimes they represented themselves as brother and sister. But invariably they were particular about the disposition of their rooms when they did not pretend to be man and wife, and in that case you could be sure that your suspicions were justified.

It was usually the man, however, who suggested any change in the rooms. The woman, with her iniquitous pretence of coy innocence, was supposed to know nothing about such sordid details. But in this case it was the woman. And she had asked that her request should be kept secret. Brother and sister, were they? Cousins, as likely as not. And she was the wicked one of the couple. It was she who was setting the snare, anyway. And what did it mean? It meant that she intended to wander into his room when the coast was clear—wander in on some pretext or another—say she had mistaken the door, or something of the sort, room 11 being next to room 10 . . . Well, it wasn't going to happen.

The manager expressed his satisfaction in a wry smile. He saw wickedness everywhere, as immoderately pious people always do, and his satisfaction sprang from the knowledge that he might throw the iniquitous into confusion. It would be a simple matter not to change the rooms, as he had been requested to do. In the morning he could say that he had been guilty of an oversight—nothing more. That would be a lie, but it would be a righteous lie, for through it the young man's soul would be saved from the siren who was trying to encompass his moral destruction. And the siren herself might conceivably get into hot water—wandering into the bedrooms of strange men in the middle of the night. For room 11 *was* occupied, though he had said it was not. And if she were to be given in charge as a prowling thief so much the better. It might reflect on the home-from-home, but if it taught the siren a lesson the balance of good would be maintained.

CHAPTER XXIII

NIGHT

THE CARD PARTY remained in session for close on two hours. Susie Landor, having done all she could in the circumstances to protect her brother, tried hard to concentrate her attention on the game. But she was more intent upon observing the other three, watching keenly for further evidence of Harold Crossland's intention to kill Eddie.

And as the minutes passed and the party maintained its cheerfulness, seeming to be animated by the most sincere spirit of friendliness, Susie wondered whether she had not dreamt all that she imagined to have taken place. She had heard of a mental state known as amnesia, in which, she understood, the sufferer was unaware of what was actually happening although he might be behaving in quite a normal manner. Perhaps she was affected by something of the sort.

But no. She must trust her own senses. There was nothing else that she could trust.

At about half-past eleven Michel Benni rose from his easy-chair and sauntered out of the room. Although he had not made a sound all the evening and had taken no notice whatsoever of the party of four at the card table, his absence was immediately felt in the room. The four of them were now alone. They, of all the guests, had not retired. The fact of its being only half-past eleven did not make their situation seem any the less isolated. With Michel Benni's going the stillness of night seemed to creep within the room, admonishing them to speak in whispers for the world was asleep.

Eddie was dealing the cards. The regular slip, slip, slip of the shiny pasteboards was the only sound—the only sound in the whole of Devonshire, it seemed.

And that tall, fair-haired young man, Harold Crossland, was going to try to kill Eddie. It was beyond all reason. Yet, why should it be beyond all reason? Susie had often read in the papers current accounts of murders, but she had always imagined murderers as people apart from the usual run of mankind. She knew they were often quite ordinary people, but she had never *felt* that they were ordinary people. Not the kind of people you meet every day. Not the kind of people you are introduced to and have meals with. Not the kind of people you became intimate with over a friendly card table.

A tiny sound disturbed the hush of the room. It was the sound of the fire falling together in the grate—a sound emblematic of sleep, of death itself.

Susie shivered. The temperature of the room seemed to sink as suddenly as the fire had sunk, and the stillness of the night became more oppressive, and one had a sense of guilt in sitting there when the world was asleep.

Steps sounded out in the dim hall. Susie looked towards the glass-panelled door at the far end of the room and saw a figure standing there, gazing within. It was the figure of a man in an overcoat and a soft felt hat that was pulled down over his ears. She recognized him as the porter. He was, no doubt, on his way to see that all the sheds and outhouses were securely fastened for the night.

"I think we really ought to be making a move," Harold Crossland murmured. "You have had your salutary departure from habit, Susie."

They had reached the Christian-name stage during the game. Susie did not mind in the least. But it was strange that they should all be so pleasantly familiar when she knew that Harold was going to try to murder her brother.

"It isn't an all-night sitting," Harold went on, "but it's an almost unheard-of departure from local custom, and that might have the same psychological effect."

"I'm perfectly satisfied," Susie remarked. "And there's Eddie yawning. You get off to bed, Eddie. Do you remember the number of your room? It's number 15."

The party rose. Eddie, by the sheer power of suggestion, wandered off first, bidding the others good night. Susie sauntered a few paces with him, murmuring a few words about the keys being in the office.

"What do you do during the day?" she then asked, turning to the others and pausing in front of the dying fire.

"There isn't a great deal to do here," Harold told her. "Where shall we go to-morrow?" he asked his sister.

"Oh, I can't make any arrangements for to-morrow," Cynthia replied. "As a matter of fact—"

She paused. Susie looked at her in some surprise.

"I may be called away to-morrow," she proceeded. "I don't know."

"Called away?" her brother echoed.

"Yes."

"Where to?"

"I don't know."

"You don't know?"

"Of course I don't know. How should I know?"

"I don't understand. Who's going to call you away?"

Cynthia did not answer. She half turned away. Her head was lowered. Susie could see that she was biting her lip, as one might who was troubled. Presently she turned back and raised her glance to her brother. Her eyes were bright. It was as though she were fighting back the tears that were causing that brightness.

Susie took a step aside and started to murmur a word or two that would enable her to withdraw as gracefully as possible from the scene. But Cynthia detained her.

"Don't go, dear," she said, while two tears did actually escape from her brimming eyes and run pathetically down her cheeks. "I shan't detain you long. Only for a moment. I have a message for Eddie. Tell him—" She paused and wiped her eyes. "Tell him," she continued, "when you see him to-morrow morning that I ask his forgiveness. We might have been very happy. Perhaps he will think of me sometimes. Perhaps I shall think of him. Though perhaps it will be better if we each try to forget. Tell him that. Tell him to try to forget. But what am I saying? To-morrow morning! . . ."

She turned abruptly away. Harold took a quick step after her and gripped her by the shoulders.

She shook herself free, violently, angrily, and moved backwards from her brother, staring at him as though with feelings of revulsion.

"Don't touch me with those hands!" she exclaimed. "Not with those hands!" Then her attitude of apparent horror fell away from her as quickly as it had been assumed. "I'm sorry, Harold," she murmured. "It isn't your fault. It isn't my fault. What is about to happen is inevitable. Think of that when the time comes. It will not be long—for you. It will soon be all over—for you. But not for me . . . Oh, let's get off to bed. Whatever can Susie be thinking of us?"

"I don't know what on earth to think," Susie stated. "Won't you tell me what's wrong? Isn't there anything I can do?"

"No, my dear," Cynthia said. "Don't think any more about it. It isn't anything—really. Come along—let's get to bed."

She was almost her normal self again as she stepped towards the door. As they ascended the stairs she was talking with a certain brightness. She said good night quite cheerily.

"They must be all mad, surely!" Susie told herself as she closed the door of her bedroom after having lighted the lamp that stood on the table in the middle of the floor.

She had closed the bedroom door because she had heard the heavy step of the porter coming up the stairs and, glancing along the corridor, had seen him extinguishing some of the lamps that were hung from the ceiling at various points.

Presently, she heard him go; then she opened her door again and looked out. The corridor was almost in darkness. The only remaining light hung over the staircase, and it had been turned very low.

CHAPTER XXIV

THE WRAP

SILENTLY SHE SLIPPED along to the door of room number 11, listened for a moment, then with infinite care put the key into the keyhole, locked the door, and withdrew the key. She guessed that if Eddie knew that she was locking him in he would be annoyed. But she could tell that he was already asleep. She could hear faint snoring.

She returned to her own room and closed the door. But she did not attempt to undress. She put on a wrap, slipping the key of room 11 into a little inner pocket. Then she stepped over to the window, feeling acutely the need for fresh air.

The window, like much that was in this place, was a museum piece. It had been fashioned for a generation that feared fresh air. It was stoutly constructed with small panes set in metal, but only the fanlight would open—and that only a few inches. The slight current of cold air, however, was sufficient to refresh Susie and to make her realize that she must keep a very firm grip upon herself.

Even now she could understand no more than she had understood at first, unless it might be that the Crossland brother and sister were thoroughly mad. And even that she could not believe. Their words and their actions could not be reasonably accounted for, yet they both had the appearance of perfectly normal human beings—rather likeable human beings. One could not think of them as being otherwise. One might regard Cynthia as a person who was unfortunately suffering from a nervous breakdown. And Harold might be in the same state. Yet, that hardly explained everything.

Eddie, at least, seemed to think that the situation was due to something of more significance than a nervous breakdown. He knew something of the truth. He had known enough, anyway, to throw that cocktail away. She was sure that he could explain all the strange words and actions if only he would speak. But he, like the other two, had pretended that the whole matter was one of no importance.

She stepped to the door and listened, listened for what she dreaded to hear—the almost soundless footsteps of a murderer moving stealthily towards his victim.

Harold's room was a little way along in the direction of the staircase. To reach room 15, in which he thought Eddie was sleeping, he had to pass her room, which was almost opposite room 15. She could hardly fail to hear even the most cautious movement. Yet, these doors were very thick and solid.

There was, of course, as she told herself, no need for her to take any further hand in the matter. She had protected Eddie by arranging for him to be put into room 11, and there was nothing else that she could do. Should Harold Crossland really mean to murder Eddie he would only creep along to room 15 and find it empty.

Still, she could not force herself to go to bed.

She opened the door a few inches and looked out. The corridor was deserted. Then she withdrew, closed the door again, and stood waiting.

But it was nerve-racking to stand there within the room, wondering whether the murderer had yet crept forth into the corridor. She opened the door a number of times, but the corridor remained deserted. If only he would make his appearance! Or if only she knew that nothing at all would happen! She could then turn in and go to sleep.

As it was, she felt that she must wait until Harold had come forth on his silent journey, had found his victim missing, and had returned to his room.

She extinguished the lamp in her own room, turning it low then blowing it out; then she opened the door a very little way. If he were to appear she could watch him, watch him enter room 15, and watch him come out again. For he might try other rooms, and if some of the doors were unlocked she must be ready to give the alarm. It would be simple enough, she reflected, and everybody was safe enough.

Then wild terror gripped her. She drew back and only the most rigid self-control prevented her from giving a scream.

The door of Harold's room had opened and Harold had stepped cautiously out. She had caught one vivid glimpse of him before she drew back out of sight, but that glimpse had told her that all the fantastic talk about murder had been grimly serious. Harold's face was white and drawn, and his expression was that of a man engaged in some fearful work. And in his hand, partly concealed by the scarlet folds of a dressing-gown he wore, there glittered the blade of a knife or dagger.

Susie's impulse was to close her door and lock it, then to scream for assistance. But she controlled herself. If this were a case of some mental disorder in Harold it would be better to avoid making a scene. He would find room 15 empty and would then, in all probability, go back to bed. And now that she knew—or suspected—what was wrong, she would force him to be put under medical supervision.

Greatly daring, she remained where she was, her door open just a fraction of an inch so that she could watch him as he entered room 15 and watch him as he came out again. And having made sure that he had returned to his room she would he able to remain at peace for the rest of the night.

She could hear his slow, slithering footsteps approaching, then gradually he came into view. She saw him move with infinite caution towards the door of room 15. He fumbled with the handle, making a slight noise. It seemed that the door was locked.

Then a surprising thing happened. The door was opened from the inside, and Eddie stood there. He had the lamp in his hand and was holding it slightly above his head as though to see the better who was there. He still had all his clothes on.

For a moment the two men stood looking at each other. Then Harold Crossland moved. He moved suddenly, quickly. He raised the hand that held the dagger and moved his feet as though poising himself for a stroke. A faint, strangled cry came from Eddie's throat, and for one awful moment his eyes opened wide in horror. But he made no move to protect himself. He seemed to be stricken with terror.

That much Susie saw before she darted forward and clutched wildly at Harold Crossland's upraised arm. Then she was aware of Eddie's coming to life. There was a violent struggle in which she just held on to Harold Crossland's arm, dragging him backwards. Eddie joined in the struggle, but, strangely, he seemed to be trying to release her grasp; he seemed to resent her interference.

Then he let the lamp fall. At the same instant Susie was thrown back against the wall of the corridor, where she stood swaying for a moment or two before she collapsed in a heap. Her last glimpse of things before she lost consciousness showed her a fierce flame springing up under the door of room 11, against which the lamp had crashed; showed her a number of half-clad people rushing to the scene; and showed her her wrap where it had fallen from her shoulders.

It was the sight of the wrap lying in the middle of the corridor that reminded her that room 11 was occupied, for she had heard faint snores coming from there. And she had locked the door and had put the key in the little pocket of the wrap.

The person inside was clamouring to be let out—shrieking piteously. The blazing oil had run under the door, and the room would quickly be an inferno. And no man could squeeze through those little windows. Harold Crossland and Eddie were throwing themselves against the door, trying to force it open.

"My wrap—" she murmured, weakly.

But they did not understand. One man picked up the wrap and with it tried to extinguish the blazing door. Then Susie gave way under the effect of the fall she had had, coupled with the effect of the smoke that was now driving everybody from the corridor. She had the sensation of being carried across somebody's shoulder down interminable stairs and out into the cold air.

It was many weeks before Susie fully grasped the significance of all that had happened. It was, in fact, many weeks before everybody else grasped it.

The fire caused the death of one man and destroyed a small part of the mansion. The man was a foreigner, named Michel Benni. But there had to be an enquiry into the cause of the fire, and certain young people who had been quarrelling and who had thus been immediately responsible for the fire were very closely interrogated. These witnesses started by giving as evidence some fantastic details about being bewitched or hypnotized or something; the specific terms did not interest the coroner particularly, for either way it was very plain that the witnesses were trying to hide the truth behind a lot of ridiculous statements that could neither be proved nor disproved. But if they thought they were going to get out of trouble by confusing the enquiry, they would soon find out their mistake. The coroner would get at the truth though he might have to keep the enquiry going every day for a month. He wasn't going to be put off with fables about men who had lived for four hundred years.

And it is possible that the enquiry might have lasted for much longer than a month had it not been for the fact that Sir Felix Quaile, the eminent psychologist, happened to return to England at that time, after a voyage round the world. Sir Felix begged eagerly to be permitted to assist at the enquiry, and the first thing he did was to state that he firmly believed that the witnesses were speaking the truth. Then he took it upon himself to prove that they were speaking the truth, and thereupon he gave an account of the almost legendary figure of Michel Benni, supporting his story with references to various authorities, some of them then living, who had proved for themselves that a man known as Michel Benni had existed continuously for at least four hundred years. This man, it was known, had brought his mind to a remarkable state of proficiency; but his mental bias had been towards the morbid, and instead of being a power for good in the world he had been a power for evil.

The persons most intimately concerned in the final stages of Michel Benni's life, Sir Felix remarked, were to be congratulated on their escape. "Not only that," he went on to say, "they are to be thanked by every healthy-minded person now living, for there can be little doubt that the man did possess the powers he claimed to possess, and no individual could call himself safe while that man remained alive."

Then Sir Felix went on to remark upon the fortunate combination of circumstances that had brought about Michel Benni's destruction. Few things could destroy him, but fire was one of those few things, and it was with satisfaction—very great satisfaction—that Sir Felix had learnt of the body's being literally burned to a cinder.

The party of four could have wished that less publicity had been given to the affair, but they had to put up with it while the proceedings lasted. Thereafter, they gladly sank into nonentity. It took three of them a long time to shake off the feeling of being haunted.

THE END

RAMBLE HOUSE's

HARRY STEPHEN KEELER WEBWORK MYSTERIES

(RH) indicates the title is available ONLY in the **RAMBLE HOUSE** edition

The Ace of Spades Murder
The Affair of the Bottled Deuce (RH)
The Amazing Web
The Barking Clock
Behind That Mask
The Book with the Orange Leaves
The Bottle with the Green Wax Seal
The Box from Japan
The Case of the Canny Killer
The Case of the Crazy Corpse (RH)
The Case of the Flying Hands (RH)
The Case of the Ivory Arrow
The Case of the Jeweled Ragpicker
The Case of the Lavender Gripsack
The Case of the Mysterious Moll
The Case of the 16 Beans
The Case of the Transparent Nude (RH)
The Case of the Transposed Legs
The Case of the Two-Headed Idiot (RH)
The Case of the Two Strange Ladies
The Circus Stealers (RH)
Cleopatra's Tears
A Copy of Beowulf (RH)
The Crimson Cube (RH)
The Face of the Man From Saturn
Find the Clock
The Five Silver Buddhas
The 4th King
The Gallows Waits, My Lord! (RH)
The Green Jade Hand
Finger! Finger!
Hangman's Nights (RH)
I, Chameleon (RH)
I Killed Lincoln at 10:13! (RH)
The Iron Ring
The Man Who Changed His Skin (RH)
The Man with the Crimson Box
The Man with the Magic Eardrums
The Man with the Wooden Spectacles
The Marceau Case
The Matilda Hunter Murder
The Monocled Monster
The Murder of London Lew
The Murdered Mathematician
The Mysterious Card (RH)
The Mysterious Ivory Ball of Wong Shing Li (RH)
The Mystery of the Fiddling Cracksman
The Peacock Fan
The Photo of Lady X (RH)
The Portrait of Jirjohn Cobb
Report on Vanessa Hewstone (RH)
Riddle of the Travelling Skull
Riddle of the Wooden Parrakeet (RH)
The Scarlet Mummy (RH)
The Search for X-Y-Z
The Sharkskin Book
Sing Sing Nights
The Six From Nowhere (RH)
The Skull of the Waltzing Clown
The Spectacles of Mr. Cagliostro
Stand By—London Calling!
The Steeltown Strangler
The Stolen Gravestone (RH)
Strange Journey (RH)
The Strange Will
The Straw Hat Murders (RH)
The Street of 1000 Eyes (RH)
Thieves' Nights
Three Novellos (RH)
The Tiger Snake
The Trap (RH)
Vagabond Nights (Defrauded Yeggman)
Vagabond Nights 2 (10 Hours)
The Vanishing Gold Truck
The Voice of the Seven Sparrows
The Washington Square Enigma
When Thief Meets Thief
The White Circle (RH)
The Wonderful Scheme of Mr. Christopher Thorne
X. Jones—of Scotland Yard
Y. Cheung, Business Detective

Keeler Related Works

A To Izzard: A Harry Stephen Keeler Companion by Fender Tucker — Articles and stories about Harry, by Harry, and in his style. Included is a compleat bibliography.

Wild About Harry: Reviews of Keeler Novels — Edited by Richard Polt & Fender Tucker — 22 reviews of works by Harry Stephen Keeler from *Keeler News.* A perfect introduction to the author.

The Keeler Keyhole Collection: Annotated newsletter rants from Harry Stephen Keeler, edited by Francis M. Nevins. Over 400 pages of incredibly personal Keeleriana.

Fakealoo — Pastiches of the style of Harry Stephen Keeler by selected demented members of the HSK Society. Updated every year with the new winner.

RAMBLE HOUSE's Other Loons

The End of It All and Other Stories — Ed Gorman's latest short story collection

Four Dancing Tuatara Press Books — *Beast or Man?* By Sean M'Guire; *The Whistling Ancestors* by Richard E. Goddard; *The Shadow on the House* and *Sorcerer's Chessmen* by Mark Hansom. With introductions by John Pelan

The Dumpling — Political murder from 1907 by Coulson Kernahan

Victims & Villains — Intriguing Sherlockiana from Derham Groves

Evidence in Blue — 1938 mystery by E. Charles Vivian

The Case of the Little Green Men — Mack Reynolds wrote this love song to sci-fi fans back in 1951 and it's now back in print.

Hell Fire — A new hard-boiled novel by Jack Moskovitz about an arsonist, an arson cop and a Nazi hooker. It isn't pretty.

Researching American-Made Toy Soldiers — A 276-page collection of a lifetime of articles by toy soldier expert Richard O'Brien

Strands of the Web: Short Stories of Harry Stephen Keeler — Edited and Introduced by Fred Cleaver

The Sam McCain Novels — Ed Gorman's terrific series includes *The Day the Music Died, Wake Up Little Susie* and *Will You Still Love Me Tomorrow?*

A Shot Rang Out — Three decades of reviews from Jon Breen

Mysterious Martin, the Master of Murder — Two versions of a strange 1912 novel by Tod Robbins about a man who writes books that can kill.

Dago Red — 22 tales of dark suspense by Bill Pronzini

The Night Remembers — A 1991 Jack Walsh mystery from Ed Gorman

Rough Cut & New, Improved Murder — Ed Gorman's first two novels

Hollywood Dreams — A novel of the Depression by Richard O'Brien

Seven Gelett Burgess Novels — *The Master of Mysteries, The White Cat, Two O'Clock Courage, Ladies in Boxes, Find the Woman, The Heart Line, The Picaroons*

The Organ Reader — A huge compilation of just about everything published in the 1971-1972 radical bay-area newspaper, *THE ORGAN*.

A Clear Path to Cross — Sharon Knowles short mystery stories by Ed Lynskey

Old Times' Sake — Short stories by James Reasoner from Mike Shayne Magazine

Freaks and Fantasies — Eerie tales by Tod Robbins, collaborator of Tod Browning on the film FREAKS.

Six Jim Harmon Double Novels — *Vixen Hollow/Celluloid Scandal, The Man Who Made Maniacs/Silent Siren, Ape Rape/Wanton Witch, Sex Burns Like Fire/Twist Session, Sudden Lust/Passion Strip, Sin Unlimited/Harlot Master, Twilight Girls/Sex Institution.* Written in the early 60s.

Marblehead: A Novel of H.P. Lovecraft — A long-lost masterpiece from Richard A. Lupoff. Published for the first time!

The Compleat Ova Hamlet — Parodies of SF authors by Richard A. Lupoff - A brand new edition with more stories and more illustrations by Trina Robbins.

The Secret Adventures of Sherlock Holmes — Three Sherlockian pastiches by the Brooklyn author/publisher, Gary Lovisi.

The Universal Holmes — Richard A. Lupoff's 2007 collection of five Holmesian pastiches and a recipe for giant rat stew.

Four Joel Townsley Rogers Novels — By the author of *The Red Right Hand: Once In a Red Moon, Lady With the Dice, The Stopped Clock, Never Leave My Bed*

Two Joel Townsley Rogers Story Collections — Night of Horror and Killing Time

Twenty Norman Berrow Novels — *The Bishop's Sword, Ghost House, Don't Go Out After Dark, Claws of the Cougar, The Smokers of Hashish, The Secret Dancer, Don't Jump Mr. Boland!, The Footprints of Satan, Fingers for Ransom, The Three Tiers of Fantasy, The Spaniard's Thumb, The Eleventh Plague, Words Have Wings, One Thrilling Night, The Lady's in Danger, It Howls at Night, The Terror in the Fog, Oil Under the Window, Murder in the Melody, The Singing Room*

The N. R. De Mexico Novels — Robert Bragg presents *Marijuana Girl, Madman on a Drum, Private Chauffeur* in one volume.

Four Chelsea Quinn Yarbro Novels featuring Charlie Moon — *Ogilvie, Tallant and Moon, Music When the Sweet Voice Dies, Poisonous Fruit* and *Dead Mice*

Five Walter S. Masterman Mysteries — *The Green Toad, The Flying Beast, The Yellow Mistletoe, The Wrong Verdict* and *The Perjured Alibi.* Fantastic impossible plots.

Two Hake Talbot Novels — *Rim of the Pit, The Hangman's Handyman.* Classic locked room mysteries.

Two Alexander Laing Novels — *The Motives of Nicholas Holtz* and *Dr. Scarlett*, stories of medical mayhem and intrigue from the 30s.

Four David Hume Novels — *Corpses Never Argue, Cemetery First Stop, Make Way for the Mourners, Eternity Here I Come*, and more to come.
Three Wade Wright Novels — *Echo of Fear, Death At Nostalgia Street* and *It Leads to Murder*, with more to come!
Eight Rupert Penny Novels — *Policeman's Holiday, Policeman's Evidence, Lucky Policeman, Policeman in Armour, Sealed Room Murder, Sweet Poison, The Talkative Policeman, She had to Have Gas* and *Cut and Run* (by Martin Tanner.)
Five Jack Mann Novels — Strange murder in the English countryside. *Gees' First Case, Nightmare Farm, Grey Shapes, The Ninth Life, The Glass Too Many.*
Seven Max Afford Novels — *Owl of Darkness, Death's Mannikins, Blood on His Hands, The Dead Are Blind, The Sheep and the Wolves, Sinners in Paradise* and *Two Locked Room Mysteries and a Ripping Yarn* by one of Australia's finest novelists.
Five Joseph Shallit Novels — *The Case of the Billion Dollar Body, Lady Don't Die on My Doorstep, Kiss the Killer, Yell Bloody Murder, Take Your Last Look.* One of America's best 50's authors.
Two Crimson Clown Novels — By Johnston McCulley, author of the Zorro novels, *The Crimson Clown* and *The Crimson Clown Again.*
The Best of 10-Story Book — edited by Chris Mikul, over 35 stories from the literary magazine Harry Stephen Keeler edited.
A Young Man's Heart — A forgotten early classic by Cornell Woolrich
The Anthony Boucher Chronicles — edited by Francis M. Nevins
Book reviews by Anthony Boucher written for the *San Francisco Chronicle,* 1942 - 1947. Essential and fascinating reading.
Muddled Mind: Complete Works of Ed Wood, Jr. — David Hayes and Hayden Davis deconstruct the life and works of a mad genius.
Gadsby — A lipogram (a novel without the letter E). Ernest Vincent Wright's last work, published in 1939 right before his death.
My First Time: The One Experience You Never Forget — Michael Birchwood — 64 true first-person narratives of how they lost it.
A Roland Daniel Double: The Signal and The Return of Wu Fang — Classic thrillers from the 30s
Murder in Shawnee — Two novels of the Alleghenies by John Douglas: *Shawnee Alley Fire* and *Haunts.*
Deep Space and other Stories — A collection of SF gems by Richard A. Lupoff
Blood Moon — The first of the Robert Payne series by Ed Gorman
The Time Armada — Fox B. Holden's 1953 SF gem.
Black River Falls — Suspense from the master, Ed Gorman
Sideslip — 1968 SF masterpiece by Ted White and Dave Van Arnam
The Triune Man — Mindscrambling science fiction from Richard A. Lupoff
Detective Duff Unravels It — Episodic mysteries by Harvey O'Higgins
Automaton — Brilliant treatise on robotics: 1928-style! By H. Stafford Hatfield
The Incredible Adventures of Rowland Hern — Rousing 1928 impossible crimes by Nicholas Olde.
Slammer Days — Two full-length prison memoirs: *Men into Beasts* (1952) by George Sylvester Viereck and *Home Away From Home* (1962) by Jack Woodford
Murder in Black and White — 1931 classic tennis whodunit by Evelyn Elder
Killer's Caress — Cary Moran's 1936 hardboiled thriller
The Golden Dagger — 1951 Scotland Yard yarn by E. R. Punshon
A Smell of Smoke — 1951 English countryside thriller by Miles Burton
Ruled By Radio — 1925 futuristic novel by Robert L. Hadfield & Frank E. Farncombe
Murder in Silk — A 1937 Yellow Peril novel of the silk trade by Ralph Trevor
The Case of the Withered Hand — 1936 potboiler by John G. Brandon
Finger-prints Never Lie — A 1939 classic detective novel by John G. Brandon
Inclination to Murder — 1966 thriller by New Zealand's Harriet Hunter
Invaders from the Dark — Classic werewolf tale from Greye La Spina
Fatal Accident — Murder by automobile, a 1936 mystery by Cecil M. Wills
The Devil Drives — A prison and lost treasure novel by Virgil Markham
Dr. Odin — Douglas Newton's 1933 potboiler comes back to life.
The Chinese Jar Mystery — Murder in the manor by John Stephen Strange, 1934
The Julius Caesar Murder Case — A classic 1935 re-telling of the assassination by Wallace Irwin that's much more fun than the Shakespeare version
West Texas War and Other Western Stories — by Gary Lovisi
The Contested Earth and Other SF Stories — A never-before published space opera and seven short stories by Jim Harmon.
Tales of the Macabre and Ordinary — Modern twisted horror by Chris Mikul, author of the *Bizarrism* series.
The Gold Star Line — Seaboard adventure from L.T. Reade and Robert Eustace.

The Werewolf vs the Vampire Woman — Hard to believe ultraviolence by either Arthur M. Scarm or Arthur M. Scram.

Black Hogan Strikes Again — Australia's Peter Renwick pens a tale of the outback.

Don Diablo: Book of a Lost Film — Two-volume treatment of a western by Paul Landres, with diagrams. Intro by Francis M. Nevins.

The Charlie Chaplin Murder Mystery — Movie hijinks by Wes D. Gehring

The Koky Comics — A collection of all of the 1978-1981 Sunday and daily comic strips by Richard O'Brien and Mort Gerberg, in two volumes.

Suzy — Another collection of comic strips from Richard O'Brien and Bob Vojtko

Dime Novels: Ramble House's 10-Cent Books — *Knife in the Dark* by Robert Leslie Bellem, *Hot Lead* and *Song of Death* by Ed Earl Repp, *A Hashish House in New York* by H.H. Kane, and five more.

Blood in a Snap — The *Finnegan's Wake* of the 21st century, by Jim Weiler

Stakeout on Millennium Drive — Award-winning Indianapolis Noir — Ian Woollen.

Dope Tales #1 — Two dope-riddled classics; *Dope Runners* by Gerald Grantham and *Death Takes the Joystick* by Phillip Condé.

Dope Tales #2 — Two more narco-classics; *The Invisible Hand* by Rex Dark and *The Smokers of Hashish* by Norman Berrow.

Dope Tales #3 — Two enchanting novels of opium by the master, Sax Rohmer. *Dope* and *The Yellow Claw.*

Tenebrae — Ernest G. Henham's 1898 horror tale brought back.

The Singular Problem of the Stygian House-Boat — Two classic tales by John Kendrick Bangs about the denizens of Hades.

Tiresias — Psychotic modern horror novel by Jonathan M. Sweet.

The One After Snelling — Kickass modern noir from Richard O'Brien.

The Sign of the Scorpion — 1935 Edmund Snell tale of oriental evil.

The House of the Vampire — 1907 poetic thriller by George S. Viereck.

An Angel in the Street — Modern hardboiled noir by Peter Genovese.

The Devil's Mistress — Scottish gothic tale by J. W. Brodie-Innes.

The Lord of Terror — 1925 mystery with master-criminal, Fantômas.

The Lady of the Terraces — 1925 adventure by E. Charles Vivian.

My Deadly Angel — 1955 Cold War drama by John Chelton

Prose Bowl — Futuristic satire — Bill Pronzini & Barry N. Malzberg .

Satan's Den Exposed — True crime in Truth or Consequences New Mexico — Award-winning journalism by the *Desert Journal*.

The Amorous Intrigues & Adventures of Aaron Burr — by Anonymous — Hot historical action.

I Stole $16,000,000 — A true story by cracksman Herbert E. Wilson.

The Black Dark Murders — Vintage 50s college murder yarn by Milt Ozaki, writing as Robert O. Saber.

Sex Slave — Potboiler of lust in the days of Cleopatra — Dion Leclerq.

You'll Die Laughing — Bruce Elliott's 1945 novel of murder at a practical joker's English countryside manor.

The Private Journal & Diary of John H. Surratt — The memoirs of the man who conspired to assassinate President Lincoln.

Dead Man Talks Too Much — Hollywood boozer by Weed Dickenson

Red Light — History of legal prostitution in Shreveport Louisiana by Eric Brock. Includes wonderful photos of the houses and the ladies.

A Snark Selection — Lewis Carroll's *The Hunting of the Snark* with two Snarkian chapters by Harry Stephen Keeler — Illustrated by Gavin L. O'Keefe.

Ripped from the Headlines! — The Jack the Ripper story as told in the newspaper articles in the *New York* and *London Times.*

Geronimo — S. M. Barrett's 1905 autobiography of a noble American.

The White Peril in the Far East — Sidney Lewis Gulick's 1905 indictment of the West and assurance that Japan would never attack the U.S.

The Compleat Calhoon — All of Fender Tucker's works: Includes *Totah Six-Pack, Weed, Women and Song* and *Tales from the Tower,* plus a CD of all of his songs.

Totah Six-Pack — Just Fender Tucker's six tales about Farmington in one sleek volume.

RAMBLE HOUSE

Fender Tucker, Prop.

www.ramblehouse.com fender@ramblehouse.com

228-826-1783 10329 Sheephead Drive, Vancleave MS 39565

www.ingramcontent.com/pod-product-compliance
Lightning Source LLC
LaVergne TN
LVHW090956080826
845145LV00003B/1024

* 9 7 8 1 6 0 5 4 3 3 4 2 4 *